HUNGER ON THE CHISHOLM TRAIL

M. ENNENBACH

DEATH'S HEAD PRESS

an imprint of Dead Sky Publishing, LLC
Miami Beach, Florida
www.deadskypublishing.com

ISBN: 978-1-63951-046-7

First Edition

Cover Art: Justin T. Coons

The "Splatter Western" logo designed
by K. Trap Jones

Book Layout: Lori Michelle
www.TheAuthorsAlley.com

ACKNOWLEDGMENTS

To Maia and Dax, you two kept me going when the world did its best to stop me. I am the luckiest father on the planet. I love you both.

To the Chris and PC3, the other two heads of Cerberus. World Domination. I couldn't have asked for better friends, writers and brothers on this journey.

To DHP, thank you for the opportunity to step outside my comfort zone. World Domination, one story at a time.

The Beta readers, who are actually all alphas in my mind. Thank you as always.

Jelly, guess what? You know exactly what I am thinking. Thank you for always expecting the best from me. For being there with a smile and making me do the same.

SUMMER, 1869 INDIAN TERRITORY

"**STRING HIM UP!** But be careful, these godless savages don't know when to quit!"

There were three of them. All covered in dust and sweat from the long chase across the plains. The heat from the sun beat down upon them as they wrestled the native youth in his buckskins to the ground and bound his arms and legs with coarse rope. The three men had an assortment of cuts and scrapes. Savage or not, the youth was scrappy. Knowing you were about to die had that effect on a person.

They dragged him to the stout old tree at the base of a low hill. The three men worked with a business-like efficiency. Even as the boy, barely into his manhood, thrashed and tried to fight while bound tightly, they took a long coil of rope and tossed it up over one of the thicker branches with a practiced motion. Then with a grunt, they begin to raise him up into the air by a loop of rope around his wrists. The old tree limb sagged a bit but held true as they tied the rest of the length around the trunk.

The not yet a man thrashed against the ropes. He looked like a butterfly seeking to escape the cocoon except for the hatred etched into his eyes. Not a sound left his mouth except for grunts of exertion. No cries.

No tears welled in his eyes even as he knew with a certainty what fate lay before him.

"Let's have us a little target practice with the Savage. Whaddya boys think?" the leader of the trio asked. A nasty smile made uglier by the scar running down his cheek broke across his leathery skin.

The others nodded. Teeth like picket fence posts, brown and crooked and spread far apart shown in their smiles. Yet for the supposed glee, the gnarled smiles never seemed to reach the fevered eyes above.

As if sensing an impending feast, a lone buzzard began to circle high in the sky. They had learned to follow men on horseback across the near-desolate plains. They always seemed to leave a trail of bloated corpses behind, either their own or anyone unfortunate enough to cross them. It watched as the men removed rifles from saddlebags strapped to too thin horses. The large bird let the thermals carry it lazily while it drifted along. As if the movement meant something, it called out into the sky that an act of egregious violence were about to occur, a second and soon third vulture arrived.

"Now then, boy, we are gonna ask you one more time. Where is the gold?" the leader snarled as his cronies aimed down the sights. The bundle just glared hatred at the men and twisted in a furious circle.

A sharp crack echoed into the air. A chunk of bark exploded off of the tree no more than a foot from the rope tied form's head.

"Damn it, Paddy! Shoot lower! You kill the Savage and we have to find another one! These red skinned bastards are like wrestling rattlesnakes! Use your damned head!" the leader growled.

"Just a warning shot to let him know we mean business," Paddy replied with what would have been chagrin on a cultured face. Instead it looked like pathetic mewling. He chomped down the cigar in his mouth as petulantly as a man that didn't know the word could, his blue eyes squinting in the sunlight.

"You ain't that good a shot and we all know it. What about that whore in Dodge? You blew off her toe tryin' to be clever." The third laughed uproariously at this. "She was hopping up and down, screaming and crying."

Paddy glared at him and spit on the ground. "You shut your mouth, Henry! I told you I saw a snake! I was trying to protect her. Not my fault she flinched when I drew."

Henry laughed even harder. "You seen her toe and thought it was some kinda snake. You surely took care of it!"

"Would you two shut your idiot mouths! Everyone knows Paddy ain't a rifleman. And that whore sure wasn't gonna get bit on the toe by a snake in the middle of town. We need to concentrate on the gold!"

"Yes, Bill. I just think Paddy ain't the one to be shooting. Remember in the war? He kept cranking that Gatling and the Union marched straight in! If he hit one, it was on accident! I do swear he is the worst shot in the entire Confederacy!"

"I killed more of those bastards in one battle than you did the entire war, you mangy son of a whore!"

Paddy swung the rifle at Henry's head with an angry cry. Henry jumped back and pulled a wicked knife from his belt. All traces of smiles were gone. They eyed each other with as much hate as the Apache boy glowered at the three of them.

"Put that knife away right now, Henry. Stop provoking Paddy. And if you swing at him again, I will let him stick that in your guts. I am so sick and tired of the two of you bickering. I'll shoot you both in the back of the skull and take the gold for myself if you don't quit!"

"Tell him to stop bringing up the whore. Every day he brings that up. There was a snake, you gotta believe me, Bill!"

Henry slid the knife back behind his belt and laughed quietly. Bill gave him a stare that foretold murder and he choked it down. "Fine. There was a snake. You done played the big hero. Too bad the Marshalls didn't see it that way. I apologize, Bill. Let's get the Savage to talk and then we can be on our way. I'm just thirsty is all. It's drier than a mule's tit out here."

A rustling in the tall dry grass was their only warning. They all turned quickly, rifles and three pistols pointed in one motion. An emaciated figure, more skeleton than human stumbled out of the prairie grass thicket. Patches of wispy long white hair clung to the skull and two sunken eyes stared in seeming incomprehension at them.

"What in tarnation is that?" Paddy cried, his finger pulling back on the trigger of his rifle a little instinctively.

Bill stared at it for a long moment. "This ain't got nothing to do with you. Best take your nearly dead self back where you came from."

The thing, clearly a person—or what was once one in better times—stopped and cocked its gaunt head at them. A hot wind began to blow and the tattered skins it had draped itself in fluttered against it. The smell of death blew oily across the space between them. Pungent enough to make eyes water, with a trace of malevolency that caused their fingers to tighten even more firmly on the triggers. It made no move to retreat or come closer. The twenty yards between the four of them seemed dangerously close. The horses whinnied in terror and all that could be seen of their eyes was white as they thrashed against the leads keeping them bound to a smaller tree. It bent against the savagery of their fear.

"I said you need to turn around and git. This is your last warning stranger," Bill muttered. His tongue felt heavy and his stomach seemed to be filled with angry hornets all of a sudden.

A soft, mournful cry came from the boy hanging from the tree. *"Wiiindeeego."*

Henry looked over his shoulder at the kid and the look of terror on his face made his bladder feel close to letting loose. He looked back and without thought pulled the trigger on his revolver. Time seemed to slow as he cocked back the hammer again. He saw the first shot hit the thing in the arm. Suddenly, all three of them were shooting. Smoke and burnt powder filled the air along with the cacophony of miniature explosions. Yet it just stood there, head cocked and watching. His bladder did release then. He felt piss run down his leg and into his boot. But he couldn't recognize it. The involuntary reaction to the creature's eyes lighting with a soft red glow took all thought from his head.

He watched as it dropped to its haunches. He saw black liquid drip from the wounds, more than he could count across its torso and limbs. Then, in a blur, it was in motion. He fumbled to reload his pistol, but his hands seemed dead. In a flash, it was on Paddy. Its claws, for there was no other way to describe those too long fingers that ended in points, tore Paddy's throat out in a single swipe. It lowered its face and drank the spewing red. If he were capable of thought, Henry may have seen the wounds as they knitted themselves closed as it drank. It sprang into the air and its mouth seemed to stretch far past the limits of a human jaw. Before Bill could get off another shot, he screamed in horror and pain. It bit through, clean through, his shoulder. Bone and flesh and muscle tore like paper. Gouts of blood rained through the air as it bit again and again, next into Bill's chest with a sickening wet rip. Henry saw ivory bone for the briefest moment before gore made everything into bubbling crimson. Then it tore out Bill's throat.

Henry knew he needed to run. To reload. To do anything but stand in his piss-soaked pants. But he couldn't will himself to do any of that. To do anything. He just stared as his two friends lay shuddering and convulsing on the dry dirt. The ground seemed as thirsty the creature, red stains where the liquid seeped into it. Then its eyes were on his. The soft glow became a bonfire of evil intent.

"Please don't," was all he could mutter. He heard the quaking in his own voice. Barely able to recognize it as his own.

The creature cocked its head again, the musculature looking more defined after it had eaten from his friends. Its jaw slowly worked. "Please don't," it whispered back to him. "Please don't." A little louder. "Please don't!" it screamed. And then it leapt at him.

The three buzzards flew above. They watched the carnage below as the one fell to its knees and feasted upon the three corpses, the sound of flesh tearing and bone cracking carrying far into the night. One by one, they drifted down and perched on the branches above the boy as he spun in circles. Fear emanated from his every pore as he too watched the thing eat until all that remained was filthy clothes and blood-stained dirt. Four sets of eyes locked upon it. Finally, the creature stood, stomach distended to the fullest extent. The body now looked healthy despite the gray pallor of the skin. Eyes burning like embers, like stars in the sky. It walked to the tree and stared at the boy for a long moment, then cocked its head. "Please don't," it said with no emotion. It reached up and, with a quick slash, the ropes were cut and the boy hit the ground with a breathtaking hiss. Then it turned and walked into the thicket of tall grass without a look back.

The boy scrambled to his feet and stared. Then he ran in the opposite direction. Only the three buzzards remained, sitting forlorn on the sagging branches of the near dead tree, cheated out of the meal they had so patiently waited for.

1

THREE YEARS LATER, ALONG THE CHISHOLM TRAIL

THE HERDS OF cattle kicked up red clouds of dust like a thundering storm sweeping across the plains. Three thousand head of cattle stomped across the open land in the eye of that storm. The setting sun still beat down mercilessly onto countryside after a long day of intense heat unbroken by a single cloud. A collared lizard sat on a large stone, unblinking as the ground rumbles underfoot. Only when one of the cattle trampled a little too close to his little kingdom did the frills on its neck expand in warning. Its lizard brain was unaware of the countless of its brethren that had been crushed under the hooves of this living force of nature as it moved slowly but surely North.

Riding carefully around the controlled chaos of the herd were six riders on sweat-slicked horses, each taking up a position to keep the stray and stubborn tons of meat on course. It was grueling in the heat and whipping dirt. Behind them rode the chuck wagon, dutifully keeping pace as the wagon bounced over every rut and rock on the trail. The remuda of spare horses followed alongside the wagon as the horse wrangler watched the placid scenery pass. It was peaceful and boring, broken by moments of sheer panic. His herd of horses, three per every man, seemed to trot happily.

The wrangler rode closer to the wagon. "Looks to be about time to stop for the night. You want to wake up the night crew, Jesse?"

Jesse looked up in surprise at him. "You darn near scared the life outta me! By God, man. Can't ya see I was lost in thought?"

"Been so long on the road staring at cow ass you have become a scholar?"

"Ain't ya got something to do? Leave me be or I will add something special to your stew! Mark my words, Jarod! You'll wish you had stayed and become a barber like your father!"

"Just wake up the night crew, ya mangy cur."

He rode away from the wagon and the angry mutters of the camp cook. He shook his head and laughed. Jesse was an odd one, but he could make the trail tack and slowly shrinking stores into a passable meal. It didn't matter if he was nearly off of his rocker from months of trail dust and the wagon rattling his brain. He listened as Jesse yelled into the back of the wagon where the night crew had spent most of the daylight sleeping.

"Time to earn yer keep! Up and at 'em!"

Two months it took to get from Texas to Kansas. Two months of fifteen mile days. The angry longhorns were easily surprised beasts and constantly on the verge of stampeding with little provocation. Get them to the Railhead, collect the money and rest for a few days before heading home again down the same heathen-infested lands. It wasn't an easy life by any means, but it was gradually getting better. In the beginning, there was nothing between home and the Railhead. But a new crop of Sooners, settlers that didn't want to wait for the official declaration from the government, had begun to build small towns along the trail. The boys didn't complain. It gave them a break, maybe a bath and night at the brothel. Beds to sleep in for a night to rest weary bones. Grazing lands with fences to keep the herd safe and full. It was damn near comfortable for a stretch.

A whistle rang out over the flat land and every head looked up in relief. Time to make camp for the evening at last. Some of the cattle trains tried to ride into the night. The cost was too high, though. Coyotes prowled the night and set the steers to stampede. Riders got thrown as horses caught hooves and broke legs. Plus, the slower pace kept the cattle weight higher and fetched a higher price at market. When all was said and done, it was the gold that mattered most. Why sacrifice to save a day or two only to return with lighter pockets?

The riders calmed the beasts into a semblance of order as the wagon made steady progress to the front of the line. Once it stopped at last with creaks and groans, four men climbed stiffly out of the back and stretched under the now bruised sky. Jarod watched them as he brought the remuda to rest farther out, where the tall grass was dancing in the wind to graze. He secured the lines of steeds and mares with enough slack to eat their fill by a slow-moving creek. More a trickle, really, but after months of no rain it wasn't wise to complain. Water was water in the middle of nowhere. He made his normal walk around the perimeter with his buck knife in hand. It didn't pay to set the horses among the snakes that liked to sleep on still warm rocks. Especially not by the only source of water that would attract prey. An errant bite could lead to a dead horse and the rest spreading far across the countryside.

As he walked, a strong scent drifted to him. He gagged as it grew stronger. Death. He knew the scent well. Something was rotting in the still hot dusk. "Damned coyotes," he muttered through clenched lips.

If the corpse of whatever it was lay in the trickling stream it could make everyone sick. So, he went against his instinct and walked into the ever-thickening cloud. He raised his eyes and looked for the telltale sign of a vulture circling overhead but saw nothing. Soon enough, the buzzing of flies led him to the source of the smell.

"Lord above," he said as he came to the grisly scene, a pile of half eaten animals, rotted and putrefying into a pool of blackened ooze in a small clearing. He stared uncomprehending at it. This was nothing normal, no creatures he had ever seen would have killed so many. Nor would they have left anything half eaten. Animals killed as necessary and ate their kills. This was something unnatural. He backed away and went to find James, the leader of the drive. This was his responsibility, not Jarod's.

2

TOWN OF DUNCAN, INDIAN REGION,
ALONG THE CHISHOLM TRAIL

"**W**AKE UP, PRISONER! Time for breakfast, you mangy prick!" the sheriff shouted has he banged on the bars of the cell. He had a scowl upon his face that was lined from years spent out in the elements. Heavy, drooping mustaches covered his mouth except for when he yelled. The folks of the new little town on the ass edge of anywhere knew he was not really as bad as he liked to carry himself, though. But that wasn't fitting for dealing with strangers.

The man on the bunk slowly stirred under the noise. He was a good-looking man with one of those age indiscriminate faces that said anywhere from thirty-five to sixty. Well groomed and dressed nicely despite the dust of the road, he was a businessman of some sort, the sheriff reckoned. But there was something about those eyes, so dark brown as to almost be black, with a glimmer that said he found everything around to be hilarious.

"Thank you kindly, Sheriff. I was hoping we could

talk reasonably this morning and you would see fit to let me loose. I'm afraid there has been a misunderstanding on a grand scale," he replied as he sat up on the edge of the bunk, putting on his most polite smile.

The sheriff stared at him with no expression. "You caused quite the ruckus last night, Mister . . . "

"Beck. Karl Beck. Please, call me Karl. And that ruckus, as you call it. Well, that was not my intention at all, I assure you."

"You spoke of consorting with demons, Mr. Beck. Willfully. Along with your talk of monsters and other tomfoolery. Why, to hear Kenzie speak of it, you would have summoned a demon right there on the spot."

Karl chuckled. "I am sure Kenzie did what she thought best, Sheriff. Her imagination may have run ahead of her reason, though. All I did was try and show a few of the patrons of the bar a few sigils in salt to ward off evil. Not summon it."

"I will be the first to admit that, on occasion, Kenzie has been known to spin a yarn or two on the quiet nights between cattle drives. But one thing she is not, Mister Beck, is a liar. Now stand up and, if you promise to remain reasonable, you can join me out here for breakfast. But no demons or I swear I will shoot the front of your skull out the back without hesitation. Do we have an understanding?"

Karl prided himself in his ability to read people and he saw the sheriff did not threaten him. He just spoke the simple truth. He nodded and stood slowly. "I appreciate the kindness. No demons, on my mother's soul, I swear."

The door to the cell opened with a squeal of metal on metal and the sheriff stood staring. "The name is Mikhail Donner. Acting sheriff until my replacement arrives from Dodge. This is just a nice quiet rest on my road to San Francisco. My brother is there, panning for gold in the hills. What brings you to our little town, Mister Beck?"

They sat at the small table in the center of the room. There were two dented plates with sausages and chopped potatoes. Before answering, Karl took two large bites of eggs. "I was travelling to Abilene from Dallas and decided to take the famous Chisholm Trail. I go where the wind takes me, Sheriff Donner. After Abilene, I shall head up to Wisconsin. A friend of mine tells interesting tales. Then perhaps to the East Coast. No real plans at all."

The sheriff nodded and ate slowly. He was a man of slow action but steady resolve. Measure twice and cut once made into a person. "Well then, as soon as the new sheriff gets here and decides what to do with you, you may just make it up to Wisconsin."

Karl made a face and swallowed as if the sausage had gone rotten in his mouth. "How long do you expect that to be? Until the new sheriff arrives, I mean."

Mikhail stared off into space. "I reckon a week or so. Shouldn't be any longer than that."

Karl nodded. "Might I have my things in the cell, then? Just my journals and such. I can use this time to record my journey so far. I've been meaning on trying to find a protégé, one to teach my tricks and help to ease the lonesome road."

Mikhail nodded. "I will need to go through it, in an effort to prevent any trouble, you see."

Karl nodded in appreciation.

"And I can sit a spell each day with you to help with the boredom I suspect. If you'd be so inclined."

"Sheriff, I would be honored." Karl was notoriously stingy with his funds and realized this was a chance to not do anything and accomplish some writing. All for free. He kept his face calm, but after the last couple months he had, this would be wonderful. Besides, he thought, the worst thing that could happen out here was a stampede or shooting. He had left the monsters behind in Dallas.

3

CHISHOLM TRAIL, CAMP SIDE

THE CAMPFIRE SENT tongues of flame into the night sky, licking the still heat and sending sparks dancing upwards toward the blanket of glittering stars above. The stew pot hung empty, scraped nearly clean by the ten ravenous men. Only Jarod and James barely ate and sat staring at the fire, the memory of the gruesome remains souring their stomachs. It had cast a pall over the normally talkative group. Even Jesse didn't mother hen the men too badly, which spoke volumes of the severity of what they had seen.

"It wasn't nothing I've ever seen. I can say that for sure. Nothing natural. Probably one of them," Thomas looked around the empty land carefully, "savages that done did it. They are barely human. Half dressed and worshipping animals. Probably like going to church to them."

Murmurs of agreement came from around the fire at his words. The saddle-sore day riders stared at the fire with drooping eyes that belied the fear they felt.

There were stories, countless stories of creatures in the night. But just as sure as the monsters of myth, the reality of the Indians and their barely concealed anger was far more real.

"They ain't all bad," Daniel muttered.

"What did you say?" Thomas asked, a bit of fire in his voice.

Daniel looked away from the flames and into the blanket of night that has settled across the land. "I said they ain't all that bad. You heard me. There's a couple of them that work the farms by me. Nice enough folk. Ain't never tried to throw no curses or nothing at me and mine. My kids play with their kids sometimes."

Sullen glares crossed the fire as the men sat a little stiffer. Timothy glared daggers at Daniel. "My entire family was nearly killed by those red skinned bastards. Nice enough folks, my ass. I'd as soon shoot my own children as let them be around any of the godless heathens."

Daniel glared right back, hand twitching slightly. "Maybe your family nearly got what they had coming to them. You ever think about that?"

"You take that back right now, you good damned fool!" Timothy shouted.

All eyes turned to Daniel. He had a burr in his saddle since they started this trek. A sour disposition that had rankled the nerves of everyone on the ride. Constantly complaining about everything one minute and arguing the next. He was the last choice for the trip, and everyone knew it. If Freddy hadn't gotten sick, he would have been left in Texas.

Daniel looked at him with a cocky grin. "And if'n I don't? What then, you ignorant sack of shit?"

Timothy leapt to his feet and dove across the fire. His hands around Daniel's throat, the two men rolled around in the dirt for a moment, scrambling to choke the life out of the other. There was no love lost between the two at the best of times. This had been boiling under the surface since the last trip to Abilene. James was content to let them fight it out for a few minutes. Maybe a black eye or two would settle them down. The others exchanged looks and a few coins were set on the ground between them. Finally, Timothy got on top of Daniel and began to rain punches down onto his face.

James stood to finally break it up when a sharp crack echoed. It took a moment for the gathered group to figure out what had happened exactly. A faint tendril of smoke rose up past Timothy's face and he looked down at Daniel's bloody face in confusion. A crimson stain grew as if a magic trick from the stained brown shirt. They could see the smoking revolver with red and yellow dancing along it's barrel in Daniel's hand. It was the source of the smoke and sound. Timothy put his hand to his stomach where the red now seemed to bubble through the rough woven fabric. He looked unseeing at the men around him. A solitary bubble of red flecked spittle formed between his lips as he took ragged wet breaths. Then he fell over, off of Daniel, onto the hard-packed ground.

Daniel stared at the body in shock. Then he dropped the revolver from shaking hands. "He was gonna kill me! You bastards saw it. He was gonna beat me to death while you all watched!" Then came great, heaving sobs as he lay under the blanket of stars.

No one said anything for a long moment, just sat watching the blood pool, nearly black, in a lake around Timothy. They were all frozen, not at the sight of death, but the suddenness of it. A howl in the distance, a wolf from the timbre of it, snapped them back to reality.

The sound of hooves galloping as well as the silhouette of Chris, the man in charge of the night crew, came into the light. He looked down at the bloody face of Daniel and Timothy's corpse. "What in the fires of hell happened?"

James felt shaky as he looked up at Chris. "A tussle that got out of hand." He turned to the others and nodded. "I need two of you to bury the body. Take his boots for his son. Bury him nice and deep, he deserves to not be picked apart by coyotes. And I need a volunteer to take Daniel to Duncan and turn him in to the sheriff."

Chad looked up. "Why take him to Duncan? We can kill him now. Justice."

Mumbles of agreement could be heard around the fire as the men stared down at the Timothy. James shook his head angrily. "I have killed before, same as all of you, I suspect. As I get older, though, I begin to worry what that does to a man's soul. Nah. I ain't God and I don't claim to speak for Him, neither. Until He sees fit to speak to me and ask me to carry out His work on Earth, I say we leave it to the sheriff to do."

Daniel gave a cry. "He was gonna kill me! I was defending myself! There ain't no reason to send me to jail for that! Ain't no crime in a man defending himself!"

James gave him a pitiless stare. "You were getting

your ass kicked. Plain and simple. And deserved. There was no reason to pull out that gun and we all know it. You'll pay for your crime, same as any of us."

Daniel groveled and tried to get to his knees, but he was pushed back down by Jarod. "Don't add to your cowardice. Accept your actions like a man."

"They'll hang me, sure as hell they will."

"No less than you deserve. I'm of a mind to shoot you where you lay myself. As is every other man around you. But James speaks wisely. And I see it this way. We shoot you, it is over. You go to Duncan, well now, you got days to ruminate on your pending death. Something feels good about that." Jarod spoke coldly and with no remorse.

Daniel looked at him with tears swelling in his eyes. He looked at the blank faces around him. Then down at the revolver in his hands. He tossed it away as if it were a coiled snake ready to strike and began to sob. "It was a mistake. An honest to God mistake. Nothing fit for a hanging."

Jarod looked at James, who nodded. A quick kick snapped Daniel's head back and all that could be seen was the whites of his eyes as the tears made rivulets down the blood on his swollen face. Lee stood and fetched a length of rope and secured Daniel's arms and legs. He nodded to James, "I reckon I'll take him to Duncan, then."

James nodded back. "Take a fresh horse. It is two days for the two of you. A week for the rest of us. Ain't no point in rushing back. Jesse'll get you enough hard tack and jerky for the trip and I'm sure you can keep yourself entertained while waiting for us to roll in."

Lee smiled for a second before his eyes fell on the

empty boots by the fire. Chad and Chris had begun dragging Timothy away from camp already. "I can find a way to keep myself occupied, I'm sure. When you boys ride in, I'll have whiskey waiting on the bar."

Jarod stared at Daniel, hatred in his inhospitable, cold, dark eyes. "I will fetch you a strong mare first thing in the morning. No use risking life and limb for a piece of shit like him."

James just stared at the ground where the blood had already soaked in. He didn't give into omens much, but this felt like a sign of things to come. The howling began again and a chill ran down his back. An ill sign indeed. "Get him out of my sight. The sooner he is hanging from the gallows, the better. The rest of you get some sleep. Our jobs got all the harder because of this son of a bitch."

The hard truth was the trail made men callous. The sun seemed to bake all of the emotion out of them, leaving nothing but grit and gristle in its place. Most had fought in the war between the States, so there was not a lot left in them, anyway. They tried to settle down and raise families and tend to the ground like their fathers, and their fathers before. But the call for more money, a better life for the kids they brought into the world was too much. It was not easy to leave home for months at a time. They had all learned death was the only thing of any certainty in this life. They accepted it as the one truth. Hard drinking and whoring was no substitute for the sacrifices they made, but for some of them, it was the only thing they had that made sense. So they found themselves under the big sky far from home with the rest of the creatures unfit to settle down.

The howling went on long into the night as the night watch kept to their rotation around the mindless herd. A fresh mound of dirt, two sticks in a makeshift cross, and an empty pair of boots were the only reminder of a fallen friend.

4

CHISHOLM TRAIL TO DUNCAN, THE NEXT EVENING

THE CHESHIRE MOON smiled down upon the lone fire burning on the shrub and grass covered plain. The Milky Way wavered in all of its glory around that mocking grin, as if God had thrown handfuls of glittering gems across the sky for all to enjoy and marvel at. Yet the magnificence of it all went ignored by the two miserable men on the uncomfortable ground below.

"You can at least untie me, let me get comfortable a little, you ungracious bastard," Daniel whined for the three hundredth time since they headed out that morning.

"I could bash your brains out and return to the cattle drive just as easily," Lee responded in mounting anger.

"You could just let me go. Tell James I managed to escape. Sweet Jesus, Lee. It was an accident. I didn't mean to kill him. It was instinct. He was about to kill me and they all just sat watching. What would you have done?"

Lee spit on the ground next to Daniel's head. "I would have taken my beating like a man. Learned the lesson of keeping my damned mouth shut. Timothy was a good man. A family man."

"So am I! Damn you! I have a wife and two kids back in Texas!"

"And if you are lucky, they will never know what a miserable prick their daddy was. Now be quiet for a damned minute or I will gag you again. Your constant chatter is giving me a headache."

Daniel's mouth moved silently a few times. His eyes shot daggers at Lee. But he thought better and kept quiet. His mouth felt chapped from wearing the gag nearly half the hard ride so far. He had begun his begging as soon as the cattle were a distant memory. Nothing he said had worked, though. His words only seemed to push Lee toward anger. After the first warning, he had gotten the handle of a revolver to the temple. When he woke, bouncing on the back of the horse, he had thrown up the little he still had in his stomach on the trail as it raced past. His ears were still ringing. After a few more hours of begging, Lee had wrapped the filthy bandana around his mouth and head. The stale salt and sweat taste had made him gag. It forced his mouth open enough that the dry air sucked all the moisture from his mouth. It had been miserable. At least his arms were tied together in front now. The strain of them being pulled behind his back had been its own hell. His legs were numb, the thick coil of rope kept his arms pinned to his side for the most part, and he couldn't get low enough to rub them and restore feeling. He could barely shove the dried strips of beef into his mouth.

Lee held up a water skin and Daniel tilted his head back to accept the piss warm dribble into his still parched throat. It was stale and tasted like the inside of a worn boot, but he didn't care. His Adam's apple bounced up and down as he swallowed every drop.

"Now I recommend you try and get some shut eye. We leave as soon as the sun rises. We should make Duncan before night fall, I suspect."

Lee stood and went to the opposite side of the small ring of stones that contained the small fire. He stretched loudly and settled down onto the ground with a saddlebag under his head. He set his hat over his face and soon began to breathe easily. Daniel watched him for a long time. The throbbing in his skull and pins and needles down his arms and legs gave him all the incentive to fight off slumber. When he was sure—as sure as he could be, at least—that Lee was asleep, he wriggled his way like a bug toward the fire. He was wrapped tightly around the legs from ankle to knee. His chest and shoulders as well. Then the last coil was around his wrists with a loop that gave some small movement but kept his forearms close to his chest. Trussed up like a prize pig on the way to slaughter, he thought to himself in fury and fear.

"Well this piggy is gonna set himself free," he whispered to himself.

He had to get close to the shimmering flames. Far closer than he preferred. Sweat instantly beaded on his forehead. He braced himself for pain and moved his wrists towards the edge of the flame. He just needed enough to burn the ropes and break his bindings. He wished he had that foul-tasting gag in his mouth to bite down on as the searing heat sent shooting pain. He watched through teared up eyes, pushing down the pain. What was a few blisters compared to swinging by the neck until dead?

Nothing. Worth it.

He would get free of his bindings. Take the horse and water skins and ride the long way around the cattle and men. He could be home, gather his family, and be on the way to California or back to Carolina before anyone was the wiser. He watched the coarse fibers of the rope as they blackened. It was miserable, slowly cooking his own flesh as the stubborn rope just smoldered. He constantly flexed his forearms, fighting against the bindings and hoping to feel them release slightly. He saw the skin on his arm slowly turn red, then angrier before bubbling slowly as he strained. The smell, like roasting pork, made him want to wretch and vomit as the pain shot lightning bolts through his arms. It grew more and more intense and he felt waves of dizziness mix with the nausea.

Then, suddenly, the charred rope flared with little dancing flames. He scooted away from the fire and mouthed silent prayers. Then he felt them loosen. His own oozing flesh seemed to help as he worked his arms free. He wanted to shout in agony and glee. But he remained quiet, watching Lee sleep a few feet away. He liked Lee. As much as any of the others was a fair assessment. He would have no second thoughts about bashing his skull open with a rock if it was that or his own life. Soon, his hands were free and he grabbed the sharpest stone he could find and began to work at the ropes around his chest and upper arms.

It was slow work. So slow through the blinding pain of the burns on his forearms. It felt like it was taking hours, that the noise of the sawing was as loud as cannon fire in the quiet night. He just needed to get his arms loose enough to reach down and free his legs. Then he could hobble his way to the horse. He chided himself to remain calm. He could taste the freedom just within his reach. He kept his mind off the pain by imagining what he would do if he could get his hands on Jarod. Fantasies of sneaking into camp and slitting his smug throat danced in his head. That would be the only thing that could make this elation better. He had always hated him. It was mutual. Pulling along the remuda, never racing off to help rein in the stampeding herd.

Then he stopped his slow cutting as a strong smell hit him like a charging steer. What was that? He had to turn his head as the beef jerky and water in his stomach came forcefully out. It smelled like the charnel pile they had found at the last camp. The one Jarod had found, but James had made him bury. He looked around frantically for the source of the stench. All seemed calm in the night. Lee remained sleeping, the hat over his face provided a mask against the smell, he reckoned. Then to his left, the shrub and tall prairie grass began to move. He sawed into the rope faster and faster. He wouldn't let a coyote take him now. Not this close to freedom. And if it woke Lee, he would never get away. He was too close.

Then he saw something crawl out of the grass. It looked human, but impossibly thin. A skeleton with gray skin barely stretched across it. As it got closer, the scent of death grew into a cloud that he could not escape. In the sudden panic of seeing that thing, he cried out. "Lee!"

Lee jerked the hat from his face and stared in alarm at Daniel. Slowly, the gears in his head turned and he realized what was happening. "You bastard!" Then his eyes followed Daniel's and he saw the living dead man slowly crawling to camp. Jagged, broken arrow shafts stuck out of its head and torso. Like a nightmare cactus corpse. The all black eyes stared with pure, malevolent intent at them. "What in God's name is that?" he asked as he pulled out his revolver.

"Death," Daniel answered. "You gotta untie me!"

Lee never turned his eyes from the thing crawling towards them. He raised his revolver and cocked back the hammer and aimed down the barrel. "Leave us be. Ain't nothing to come from this but pain."

Daniel looked at him in shock. "Don't talk to it! Shoot!"

Lee squeezed the trigger. The gun let out a small burst of fire and the bullet flew true into one of the black eyes. It looked like tar erupted from the now ruined socket and the thing fell unmoving to the dirt.

"What was that thing?" Lee asked quietly.

"Something from hell."

Lee turned to face Daniel. "Don't think your good deed of waking me earns a reprieve. You did it to save your own sorry hide as much as anything. I should have left you over the back of the horse."

"And you'd be just as dead as I'm fixing to be."

Lee turned his gaze back to the rotting corpse. He nodded once. "You may be right on that account."

"Untie me, then. We can ride to Duncan. I'll go my way, you wait for the guys."

Lee eyed him. "We just forget the incident at camp?"

Daniel nodded. "Bygones be bygones."

"Pleeeeease don't . . . "

They both gave a jump. The thing was staring balefully with its remaining eye.

"That's not possible . . . " Lee just stared at it.

A sick sound came from Daniel's throat. One of fear and utter hopelessness.

Then the thing moved with speed that should not have been possible for such a broken form. Like a cockroach, it scurried across the ground in a blur. Lee fired, but it moved so quickly he missed three of four shots. Then it was on Daniel, sick ripping sounds as its mouth tore at his stomach. Lee tried to pull back the hammer as a spray of blood fountained into air. Daniel screamed in agony with his head thrown back to face that smiling curve of the moon shining down. The creature had its head buried in his open torso. As Lee watched, the broken arrow shafts popped out of the gray flesh. The gaunt form seemed to grow as it consumed Daniel. The revolver fell from his hands as Daniel shuddered into silence, blank eyes glaring at the sky. The creature turned to stare at him. The clatter of the gun on the ground seemed to remind it of his presence.

Two black eyes stared at him out of that demonic skeletal face covered in gore. *"Pleeeease . . . "*

Lee darted toward the horse, forgotten to the side of camp. It reared in fear at the creature and all smothering smell of death. He reached for the tether tied carefully to an old withered stump. He didn't look back. Didn't want to see if the creature followed or had puts its face back into Daniel's body. The horse reared again and a metal shod hood caught him in the shoulder. He felt bone break as he spun through the air and landed with a thump and bounced on the hard packed dirt to rest with his back against the stump. Pain flared down his arm. He watched as the horse bolted into the flat lands, galloping and leaving a trail like smoke behind it.

"... don't."

He blinked and looked up through the haze in his head. The thing stood in front of him. The skin stretched over ropy muscle and seemed to be at the verge of splitting. The head cocked as it stared down at him, as if trying to figure out exactly what it looked down upon. Lee knew the answer at that moment. It was looking at its next meal. He mouthed a prayer, that the Lord watch over him in this moment of need. Then it cried out and he saw too long claws flying towards his face. Before consciousness faded, he felt his own eyes rupture like overripe berries. A thick jelly rolled down his cheeks. And all he could do was scream as he felt teeth and fetid breath upon his flesh. He screamed for a long while into the night. And then, mercifully, the night fell silent again.

The curved snarl of the moon, no smile in the face of the carnage it had witnessed, slowly lowered from its perch. Excusing itself from the horror it had witnessed. The twinkling stars winked out as the sun rose in the Eastern sky. Two dark stains and a discarded revolver by the burned-out fire were the only sign of what occurred the night before.

5

DUNCAN

THE TOWN OF Duncan had just begun to wake from the long night into another sleepy day. Barely established three years prior, it was more a collection of people looking to be lost than a real town. It came more to life when the cattle drives rolled in, or the cattlemen made the last stop as they returned to Texas. Between, it was nearly idyllic. A place to rest, to find yourself, and to share the protection of like-minded folk from the hazards of the untamed West.

Karl sat at the table in the middle of the sheriff's office. The iron barred door to his cell was hanging open behind him as he drank a cup of coffee and watched the city outside. There was a cattle drive due to arrive around the end of the week and everyone was rushing about to be prepared. It was the first of the season and a sign of times to come. As he sat there, rereading his notes on the skirmish he had stumbled onto in New Orleans, the door to the office slammed open.

He looked up in surprise. A man in tattered clothes with a few days of growth on his face stared at him with intense eyes. Karl stared back at him in curiosity. The man looked around, a bit of panic in his steely gaze.

"What year is it?"

Karl raised an eyebrow. "Eighteen seventy-two."

The man looked shocked at this. "Eighteen seventy-two? Gods be damned," he muttered. "You the sheriff round these parts?"

Karl laughed and the man gave him a cold stare. "Afraid not. Just a traveler, much like yourself if I had to guess. Name's Karl, Karl Beck. You lost, friend?"

The man gave a mirthless laugh. "You have no idea. Call me James Dee."

He extended his hand across the table. Karl shook it and was surprised to feel the callused grip. A dangerous man with killing etched onto his face. Karl grabbed the bottle of whiskey off of the floor and held it up to James. He nodded gratefully, pulled the cork out with his teeth and took a long pull. He held it out, but Karl shook his head and gestured for him to keep it. James raised it again and drained the rest of it.

"Thank you kindly, Karl."

"Of course. You seemed to have a thirst. The road does that to man."

"Where is this?" James asked, looking out the window as Tracey opened up the shop across the street. They both stared at her as she raised the blind on the door. She looked back at them and raised her hand to wave hello, but after she saw the look on both of their faces, thought better and quickly moved back further in.

"Duncan. You're in the Indian Region, smack dab in the middle of the Chisholm Trail."

James stared at him, his mouth moving soundlessly. "Oklahoma, then," he finally uttered.

It was Karl's turn to look confused. A thousand questions ran through his mind. Before he could pry one from the pack, James smashed his fist down onto the sturdy table.

"I need to get to Dust, I've got business to settle there."

"Dust?"

James looked at him with a gaze that nearly froze the blood in Karl's veins. "Dust, Texas."

Karl screwed his face up in thought. "There are so many new settlements that spring up. I can't say I recall any Dust, though. Describes most of them, though."

Neither man laughed at this half-hearted joke. James sat down in the empty chair and cradled his face in hands. Karl watched him warily. He knew the look of a man with a mission. And of a man lost. In his experience, that made for one dangerous combination.

"What's your business in Dust, if you don't mind me asking, Mr. Dee?"

"You wouldn't believe me if I told you, Mr. Beck. You'd think I was crazy. Which way is Texas?"

Karl smiled. "You may find yourself surprised at what I would believe. But if you head out and take a right and keep going for a mighty long spell, you'll reach Texas. Just follow the Chisholm Trail."

James Dee stood and offered his hand again, which Karl shook. "I thank you for the drink and the directions. I'm off to find Dust then, as soon as I can. I have Gods to kill." With that, he turned and left. Karl sat staring long after the stranger had turned and begun to walk down the street.

Mikhail walked in moments later and saw Karl still staring into space. "Did you see the stranger?" News travels fast in a small town.

"I did."

"And? I hear he already began to head out of town."

"He needed directions is all."

"You look a might bit disturbed. Was he trouble?"

Karl gave him a long, steady look. Then he reached down and grabbed a fresh bottle of whiskey. "Like you would not believe. He is headed to Texas. And I fear he brings Hell with him."

Mikhail stared at the normally unflappable Karl Beck. "That bad?"

Karl poured three fingers into the dented metal coffee mug and threw it back in one drink. "Worse for whoever it is he is after."

They sat quietly for a long spell. Mikhail grabbed the bottle and poured himself a glass as well while the wind blew down the main street of the one-road town. Karl stared out the window. Tracey busied herself with moving the stock around on the shelves across the street. She was a fine-looking lady, if a bit withdrawn from the rest of the townsfolk.

"What's her story?" he asked as he refilled each mug from the bottle.

Mikhail turned and looked. "Tracey? English from South something or other. Was married once upon a time. Real bastard, I hear. She had about enough of him and hopped a boat. Then kept on moving until she finally found Duncan."

Karl nodded. He couldn't think of a better place to be lost and found. "She hasn't said two words to me."

Mikhail laughed. "Spend some money and she'll thank you kindly. She's a tough one. Rumor has it she has taken to the Laudanum. I can't say for certain. Until it becomes a problem for the rest of the townsfolk, it doesn't matter none. So tell me, this demon stuff, what's your real profession?"

Karl took a long sip of his whiskey. Thoughts of James Dee raced through his mind. "I don't think you'd believe me."

"Try me. I've been told I am a good judge of character, part of the job I reckon. You don't strike me as the sort to consort with the darkness."

Karl smiled, one that didn't seem to quite reach his eyes as he stared outside. "Fine. What if I told you that monsters were real? Really real? And that some of us have taken it upon themselves to stop them?"

"I would question if you were right in the head. Are you saying they are real? You're one of those people?"

"I have crisscrossed this young nation of ours over the last twenty-five years doing just that. Seen things that would make you sleep with a lantern burning next to your bed. Stopped events that could have probably ended everything more than a few times."

Mikhail sat silent for a moment, watching Karl's face. "And that brought you here? Some kind of monster?"

Karl laughed. "No. Treasure brought me to Texas. A monster in New Orleans knocked me off course.

And I decided to head up North to lick my wounds and study some more."

"Treasure?"

"If the rumors are true, luck itself. Somewhere in the Southwest. The power to harness it, bend it to your will."

"You want to be lucky? All of this to be good at cards?"

Karl shook his head sadly. "No. I just don't want the wrong people to find it. It isn't a curse I want for myself at all. There are stories of the end of all things. In these tales, they talk of one person that can stop it with the power of luck."

"Could it have been the stranger from earlier?"

"No. He has his own fate, his own path to walk. I have a feeling I have to find the right person before I can find the treasure I seek. I just have no idea where to look. So, it's to Wisconsin to chase rumors. Then back to the Northeast to restock."

"Sounds lonely, what with saving the world from monsters and no one knowing."

Karl gave him a steady look. Then removed his jacket and rolled up his sleeve. Three puckered scars traveled up his arm, deep looking rents that must have been clear to the bone. "The thing that did this to me killed my wife. My pregnant wife. If loneliness is the price to pay to stop some creature from doing this to another, that is a price I will gladly pay."

Mikhail stared in shock at the scars. Nothing short of one them big cats he heard came around with traveling shows could have done that. Yet part of him knew it was no big cat. The same part of him that believed Karl even if it was the most outlandish thing he had ever heard. "So the wards you drew in salt at the bar were just that?"

"Simple things to keep lesser spirits at bay. Nothing more."

"You realize you are free to go, don't you? Have been since the second day. It's why I don't lock the cell at night."

"I do. But I have some things to sort out. And your hospitality is second to none, Sheriff."

Mikhail smiled. "You're welcome to stay until my replacement comes. Might be a tad hard to explain you loitering in the cell after that. Why don't you come to my place tomorrow evening? Have a real dinner. My wife is an excellent cook and we'd both be happy to have you."

Karl blinked in confusion. "Someone married you? On purpose?"

"Now I expect you to have better manners than that. Jia-Li doesn't tolerate tomfoolery."

"Jia-Li? Your wife is Chinese?"

"That she is. The most beautiful flower of the Orient, if I do say so myself. Came with her father as the transcontinental railroad was being built. We met in the north. Love at first sight. For me, anyway. She couldn't speak a lick of English and her daddy couldn't stand me. But I have a pernicious streak a mile wide. So here we are after ten years."

Karl smiled. "I think I would be honored to meet your lovely wife. I shall be there."

"You bring the whiskey."

"Deal."

Mikhail stood up and adjusted his belt and looked outside the window. Tracey smiled and waved and he tipped his hat to her. "Time to make the rounds. You want to take a stroll with me? Everyone is a might bit curious as to who the stranger is that sits in the jail all day and summons demons."

Karl shrugged. "Why not? It ain't like I'm accomplishing much here. This belly full of whiskey could use walked off if I plan on making it to sunset." He grabbed his battered hat off the hook and shrugged on his just as beat jacket.

Together they walked across the street and into the town store. Tracey gave them both a smile and curtsey. "Morning, Sheriff. And a good morning to you, Mr. Beck. I've seen you sitting in the sheriff's office, wondered if you would ever venture across the street and say hello."

Karl smiled at her and removed his hat. "I reckon it was odd seeing me look out across the bustling main street the last couple days. Us hardened criminals know when we need to stay put, though. A pleasure to meet you."

Mikhail stood to the side, pretending to look at the wares as they made their introductions. "Karl is a rehabilitated man, Tracey. He just needed a few days in jail to see the error of his ways."

She raised an eyebrow. "Rehabilitated? Seems like there is still a bit of scoundrel behind his eyes. I hear you like to play with demons, Mr. Beck. Any truth to that?"

"In my experience, there is no playing with demons. You either send them back to Hell, or they kill you. I ain't been killed yet, as fortune would have it. Not for lack of trying on their part. I fear the rumors may have been exaggerated slightly, ma'am."

She gave a quizzical glance at Mikhail who only shrugged. "You strike me as an interesting man, Mr. Beck. Possibly dangerous, as well."

"Part of my charm, I suspect."

"Karl will be joining my wife and I for dinner tomorrow. He is in charge of bringing the whiskey. Make sure he buys a bottle of the good stuff, won't you?"

"Aye. The special reserves."

"You know you're more than welcome to join us as well. Just a quiet night of good food and conversation. Jia-Li would love to have a lady to converse with."

Tracey eyed Karl up and down. "I just might. The store is as ready as it is going to be for the Drive. The first of many if we are lucky."

"Well then, Karl will be back tomorrow for the whiskey and he can escort you to dinner. The street can be filled with danger and all that."

She smiled and nodded. "How refreshing to have a gentleman escort me through town. You lads have a good day. And I will see you tomorrow, Mr. Beck."

Karl smiled back and bowed slightly. "Yes, ma'am."

Her eyes lingered on them long after they had left her store. A wistful smile sat upon her lips for a few moments only to be replaced with a dour expression. She shook her head and went behind the counter and gave a careful look outside. Then she removed a tall green bottle and inserted a glass straw. She covered the end with her finger and pulled it out, now nearly full, and let it drain into the glass of water she kept by her register. She slowly stirred it with the glass straw, still looking outside with that same expression stuck upon her lovely if gaunt face. She took a long drink of the concoction and soon, a dream peace flowed across her. "I will have to find an excuse to not go tomorrow," she slightly slurred into the empty store.

Karl and Mikhail made their round from one end of the street to the other. They stopped in and said hello to the townsfolk that readied themselves for the cattle drive. Cody, the local sawbones, busied himself by soaking his implements in carbolic acid.

"It's the latest thing," he proudly announced. "Dr. Lister in Scotland has published a new study on the affect of sterilizing and how it has led to fewer infections."

Mikhail nodded, apparently having heard this speech countless times before. But Karl was intrigued. "So you spray them with the acid to kill the infection carrying germs?"

Cody nodded excitedly. "It will be all the rage soon enough. Disinfecting the surgical tools will save countless lives. He also recommends washing your hands quite often to prevent the introduction of new infection. Revolutionary! It's only been six years since his study was released, but the lives saved have already been countless."

Karl was about to ask more when a commotion outside got his attention.

"Godless Savages! Each and every last one of you!"

He and Mikhail hurried out to see two Natives being confronted by an angry man dressed in all black. "Hasse Ola and River Dixon, the tax collectors for the tribes. The man in black is the preacher, Josiah Long. We better stop this before it escalates," Mikhail muttered.

HUNGER ON THE CHISHOLM TRAIL

The preacher was red faced and kicking dirt at the two tall Natives. "Filthy red skinned bastards! If'n you won't accept the word of Lord and Savior, the fires of eternal damnation await your immortal souls!"

The younger of the two, Hasse Ola, stood calmly watching Josiah. River, on the other hand, looked like a storm cloud about to burst. "My people have seen the love and saving of your Lord. His grace pushed my people off of our sacred lands. Now this dust bowl is our legacy until he decides to push again. I will remind you, you are guests on our land, preacher. It is by our kindness you are allowed to stay."

"And the collection you make off of every head of cattle that comes through. Don't act as if you and your people are doing us a kindness!" Josiah spat the words into the dry air.

"What seems to be the problem out here, Josiah?" Mikhail interjected himself.

Josiah turned and the red dimmed a little. "I am trying to save the souls of these filthy heathens, sheriff. That is all. Doing my duty as a man of God."

Mikhail snorted. "And what were you preaching last night at Kenzie's? Was that the gospel of drinking too much and consorting with whores?"

"I did no such thing. I may have enjoyed a glass or two of brandy while extoling the virtues of God. But that is no sin, I assure you. And I may have had a private discussion with Tara on the matters of sin. As the Lord himself saw fit to charge me to do."

"Leave River and Hasse Ola alone. He is right. We are here at their discretion."

"But . . . "

"I am not asking, Josiah."

Josiah gave an angry glare at the two Natives before stomping off toward the bar. River gave Mikhail a friendly nod. "Much appreciated, Sheriff. Cattle should be here in a few days. Much celebration and excitement, I am sure."

Mikhail smiled back. "My last one in Duncan. I expect my replacement any day now. River, Hasse, allow me to introduce you to Karl Beck. Karl is a visitor resting up after a long trip."

Hasse Ola gave Karl a steady look and then signed something to River who nodded. Karl watched them carefully, trying to decipher the signals. "A pleasure to meet you both."

River looked to Hasse Ola who gestured more. "Hasse Ola says you have strong medicine. The taint of great dark has been washed away by your hands. It is an honor to meet you, Karl Beck."

Karl looked surprised. "The tribal hand talk, I've heard of it but never witnessed it myself. The honor is all mine."

River looked pleased. "Feel free to come by our toll collection office anytime. We can discuss your medicine in detail."

"I would be honored. I have plenty of questions for you both, if you'd be willing to answer them. It isn't often a Cherokee and a Muscogee—if I'm not mistaken—work together. At least not from what I have read."

Hasse Ole signaled more and River watched. "He is impressed a white man can tell our tribes apart. To most, we are one group of savages."

Karl smiled. "Most white men are idiots, as near as I can tell."

River laughed. "It seems to be an affliction all men are susceptible to."

Mikhail clapped his hand as he laughed. "It warms the heart to see two Savages and a man that consorts with demons hitting it off right away. It truly does."

Hasse Ola signaled and River laughed and shook his head. "He says it is funny that two pale faces can nearly hold a civilized conversation. The elders will tell of this in the sweat lodge for years to come."

Karl looked at them both deadpan. "I'm still amazed someone married this lout. And now I see he is friendly with the Natives. No one will believe it back East either."

The four men, so different, laughed and joked as the sun baked down relentlessly above them. A small mouse sat in the shade by the Cody's small office and watched them curiously. It held a seed to its mouth and gnawed contentedly. For a moment, everything was fine in Duncan. Peace seemed to ebb across the nearly empty street with the faint hot breeze that blew up from the South. The mouse and the men sat unconcerned as the world rolled on into the afternoon. That was when the rattlesnake opened its impossibly wide mouth and lashed out. Its fangs piercing the mouse along its side, it fell over as the venom coursed through, convulsing yet still conscious enough to feel pain. The snake didn't care for peace. It hungered and the mouse was a perfect snack. The men parted with smiles and hands raised in waves. The snake coiled happily and ate the mouse whole. The West could be beautiful, as long as the untamed was respected.

6

CHISHOLM TRAIL

"**WHAT'S THE GODDAMNED** point in riding ahead of the drive if you ain't gonna watch for snakes on the trail?" James yelled for the third time in as many minutes.

Everyone was soaked with sweat and covered with dust from the stampede. Chad stood next to his horse staring at the ground in silence.

"We lost fifteen steers! Fifteen! That's coming out of your share, cause I'll be damned if I'm taking a loss because you couldn't do the one thing you were brought along to do!"

The day had started off well. Even down three bodies they had managed to keep everything moving slowly the day before. But today had been a series of bad luck. A snake lashed out and bit one of the cattle and it had bellowed in pain and surprise. The rest had taken the call of danger to heart and scattered in three directions. The skeleton crew managed to wrangle most of them in and get them to calm again. But fifteen had charged blindly across the arid landscape.

HUNGER ON THE CHISHOLM TRAIL

Too close to the deep ravine, the force of fifteen tons stomping had proven too much for the ground. In a matter of seconds, it gave way. The cattle had fallen the fifty or so feet down to hit the bottom with jarring thuds that broke bones and necks. James had taken it upon himself to shoot each of the poor creatures that lay baying in agony.

Each shot was the grand total of the trip lowering by four dollars. Sixty dollars was nothing in comparison to the roughly twenty-nine hundred heads they still had, but it was a black mark on his leadership. One that would be remembered when the next cattle drive was ready. That and the loss of a man—while not uncommon—was enough to give him the sinking suspicion this would be his last drive as team leader.

He didn't even know if he cared as much as his screaming at Chad dictated. Hell, it was Chad's second drive. And the snakes survived by blending in. But someone had to take the brunt of his anger. He had been boiling up too. Timothy was a friend. And that bastard Daniel had put him down because he couldn't keep his smart mouth quiet.

"I'm sorry, Boss. I don't know how I missed it. I already had gotten three rattlers this morning."

James looked at him and his anger finally burned out. "It happens. Don't let it happen again, alright? Tell the boys we are breaking for camp early. And tell Jesse to get the stew going and not to be so stingy with the meat and onions. It was damn near brown water yesterday. I know he is stretching the goods, but Duncan is a few days out. Lee probably got there today and is giving the whores a thorough checking. Go!"

Chad managed a smile, got back in the saddle, and rode to tell the rest the good news. James watched for a second and nearly smiled. He wasn't always so dour. But things had felt off about this trip from the start. His mother always had feelings that nine times out of ten turned out to be true. He had as well. Intuition, his father had called it. He just wished the intuition didn't make him feel like the bad was only going to get worse.

"Boss!" Chris called out, interrupting his dreary thoughts. "I think you might want to come see this."

James rubbed his eyes. "What in tarnation is it? Don't tell me we lost another heifer."

He saw the look on Chris's face and that sinking feeling began to free fall in his guts. He liked Chris. The man could chew the fat with nearly anyone and still manage to keep both the men and the herd on track. He usually had a sparkle of mischief in his eyes. Not now, though. Now he stood off from the makeshift camp Jesse was setting up. He resigned himself to more bad news and walked over to see what fresh hell awaited.

"What is it? Let me warn you, I'm about out of my tolerance for bad news. That god forsaken rattler already cost us sixty dollars. On top of everything else, I'm starting to think we are cursed."

Chris stood by a ring of charred rocks. A campfire seemed to be a likely guess. "It's not too old boss. I'm guessing Daniel and Lee."

James stared at it in bewilderment. "You called me over for this? It was a matter of time until we showed up to one of their campsites."

Chris made a sour face. "It was indeed. I called you over because of this."

46

He beckoned James closer and pointed down at a deep red stain in the ground. Then to another. "Looks like there was a struggle and someone got hurt pretty bad. And that isn't all. I found this as well."

He held up a revolver. James grabbed it and gave it a once over. "Fired multiple times."

Chris nodded and bent down by the remains of the fire, as if trying to suss out what had happened. "If Daniel tried to escape and Lee was forced to draw on him . . . "

"There seems to be enough blood for a fatal shot," James finished. "Do you smell that?"

Chris gave a shudder. "Just like at camp the other day."

They pushed about in the tall grass looking for another pile of animal carcasses. James let out a whistle and Chris walked over to see what had caught the Boss's attention. There was a smear of black on the ground. Like tar almost. And where it had dripped, the grass was dead.

"I don't like this. Not one bit," Chris mumbled. He reached up to his neck and wrapped his hand around the silver cross he wore. He was the first to tell a salacious joke with the rest of the guys. But he was also the first to attend service in whatever town they had ridden into. A good man, comfortable in his own skin and faith.

"Damn it all to Hell. As much as the bastard deserved the trip to the gallows, a gut shot in the middle of nowhere is a bad end. And now this black shit. What in the world is going on?" James stared at the ground with a haunted expression.

"It feels like this trip is tainted."

James looked at Chris and shook his head. "Mumbo Jumbo. Ain't no such thing as curses. Just plum bad luck. We'll know well enough in a couple days when we get to Duncan. Until then, let's keep this between us. No need starting a panic. Everyone is heavy hearted enough with the loss of Timothy."

Chris gave him a deeply concerned look. But he saw the logic of the plan. He eventually shrugged his shoulders. "Fair enough."

"What brought you over here, anyway?"

Chris looked away, a hint of red on his wind burnt cheeks. "We just woke up and I had the need for my evening constitutional. All them beans in the stew Back of the wagon smells like something . . . " He trailed off as he looked back at the stained dirt. "It smells awful."

Neither man smiled. In the distance, a wolf howled as night fell over land. They both shuddered.

Jarod stood a ways off, watching the two speak. He wondered at what could have pulled them over there to talk. He shrugged and set up the remuda for a night's grazing, brushing the horses and lost in his own thought. They were close to Duncan, close to the blue-eyed gal at the local bar/brothel. He'd planned on stopping the last time through but then he met her. Tara. Half Indian, her father was from a tribe far to the North. When he died, she and her mother had made their way steadily South. Eventually, she had settled in Duncan. And he had fallen for her. After the herd was delivered to Abilene, he planned on buying a ring and proposing to her. He knew he was getting long in the tooth, but he had a grant in Texas. And she had the prettiest eyes. If she accepted, he was going to retire from this game. Set up shop and start growing something on his five-acre plot. Maybe raise a family. Who could say?

Jesse had the cook pot over the flames and was busying himself to chopping onions and carrots. James had said not to be stingy, so he broke into his reserves and put two diced up pieces of salt bacon in. Some peppers he had gotten in trade from the Spanish that rode through on occasion as well. They would feast tonight. He paused and thought about Timothy and shook his head. A damn shame. A good man. And he hardly ever complained about what was in the pot for dinner. He heard the others whispering about the run being cursed and just shook head.

"You fools got time to gossip like old biddies, you got time to set up camp. We didn't break early so you could lollygag."

The guys grumbled but went about the routine. Chris came walking back with James, both men looking sour but trying to squeeze fake smiles on. Chris grabbed Mitch, Paulie, and Danny and they took a circuit around the cattle. It was quiet except for the wolf in the distance. After the excitement of the day, even the herd was exhausted, content to stand and eat the tall grass while the men waited for the stew to finish. The sky went from deep orange to purple as they set up. No one mentioned the half speed everyone else seemed to be moving at.

Soon enough, the food was ready and Jesse clanged the triangle of metal with one of his oversized spoons. The men ambled into a line, each holding a dented deep plate and a spoon. They made their way past Jesse and settled down with the evening feast. It was quiet except for spoons dragging across metal. No one felt up to banter.

Finally, Chad spoke up, "How far outta Duncan are we, boss?"

James looked at the stars for a moment. "We lost most of today. I reckon three more days. Barring any unforeseen accidents, we will be elbows deep in whiskey and whores before we know it."

A round of laughter greeted that. James didn't allow liquor on the trail except one bottle Jesse kept hidden away. Emergency whiskey, they called it. Injuries weren't unheard of on the trail, something to numb the pain in that case was prudent. And if Jesse snuck a nip once in a while, well, James never mentioned it. Sitting on that damned wagon all day did things to man's back. He didn't come by his natural good humor without a little something to keep him from screaming all day.

The four night's men took turns patrolling the herd and eating. They had lanterns hanging off their saddles. Once all four had gotten a turn, they waved to the day crew and set out on their paces. Soon, a second wolf began to howl, answering the first in its lonesome call. The Milky Way hung above, obscured by a fast-moving system coming in from the East.

"We might get a little rain tonight. You boys got your oiled leathers?" Paulie asked.

Danny stared hard at the clouds. "Ain't gonna be no rain. Not as fast as it is blowing. Almanac says no rain for weeks."

"You and that gosh darned Almanac," Mitch chided. "About as reliable as Paulie in a fight!"

"I stood a sight better than you the last time it

came to fisticuffs. You were so drunk that the purdy lady, what was her name? Anyway, she knocked you down right quick. You never got back up once!"

"Kenzie. That purdy lady runs the brothel. And she has a Derringer and three knives on her at all times. I stayed down because she was gonna shoot if I moved."

The four of them laughed. On their second run last year, there ended up being five different runs meeting in Duncan at once. Everything was going great until the drinking commenced for real. Mitch was playing faro with some of the other crews. Mitch was a good guy. A great worker that never gave up. But his mouth had been known to get his and the rest of the crew's rears into the fire. His mouth was the only thing quicker than his draw. Which could be unfortunate, as his pistol was usually just as fast to be used once he started losing at cards.

It was a pretty stout ruckus that evening. Little damage to the establishment, less to each other. Just a few black eyes, along with some new friends. It was fortunate that the madam, Kenzie, had kept Mitch still. It could have escalated quickly from a regular brawl to calling the undertaker.

A third howl rang out. This one sending shivers down the entire camp's back. A hollow note of fear tinged it as it filled the night. A few of the steer jerked awake at it. The air became filled with fine grit as the winds picked up.

"Let's keep the cattle still. Ride out," Chris said as jagged lines of purple lightning flashed across the sky like branding irons.

The men rode with small circles of light from the

hammered lanterns flickering across the dark flat land. The wind fought to extinguish the glow. Chris rode in the back of the pack and watched as Danny's went out. Then Paulie's. Soon, only his and Mitch's fought against the night. A triple prong of electricity raced across the sky as a rumble of thunder, near subsonic rattled the ground.

"Boss, they look ready to run!" Mitch called out.

Then a bolt of fire sizzled to the ground not a mile away. The after image burned itself into Chris's eyes as his horse reared back in surprise. He found himself falling toward the ground and willed himself to go limp. As the hard-packed earth hit his back, his breath was launched out in a fierce exhalation. But all he could think as it happened was, he thought he saw the shape of a person loping across the ground toward them.

He scrambled to his feet in time to see the bouncing light of Mitch's lantern dance forward as the ground rumbled beneath him. "Stampede! All Hands!!" he screamed into the night as the world became chaos.

He saw the men roll off the ground around the fire that sputtered weakly against the winds, the embers flaring. Soon they all had their lanterns going, the beams dancing in the air. Chris got back onto his horse, not bothering to relight his torch. The need to get the cattle calmed down overrode any sense of safety. For a moment, one of the stray beams flashed on to Paulie's back as he raised a lasso to pull in a steer. It flashed back and, again, Chris thought he saw that person. Too quickly the light moved. A muffled cry in the cacophony caught the breeze. The light came back to show Paulie no longer in the saddle. Chris knew how perilous this could be. The herd couldn't see any better than he could. And sheer terror from the lightning flashing closer and closer meant they were heedless to a possible body in their path.

"Paulie!!!!" he shouted. The wind and stampede drowned out his voice. He urged his mare, still wide eyed but well trained, toward where he had seen Paulie last. He combed the ground looking for any trace of his friend.

The sky flashed above him, illuminating the night briefly. He saw a pool of what could have been blood. The ground rumbled with thunder and hooves. He counted to five and kept his eyes trained for Paulie. Another flash. He was positive what he had seen was blood. But no body.

Time seemed to slow around him as the stench of lingering death hit him in the face. He felt as if he existed a step out of time as he watched the chaos around him in brief moments of clarity.

He heard Mitch calling out to try and calm the rumbling herd. Flash. He could make out Mitch riding. Flash. There was something else. That person he believed he saw. A rail thin body. It was perched on the sweeping horns of a terrified steer. Impossible.

Flash.

The gaunt form leapt off of the rack into the air toward Mitch. A cry choked itself out in his throat, a warning he couldn't get out.

Flash. Mitch's horse galloping rider-less. Just like Paulie's.

He drove his heels into the flanks of his mare,

toward where Mitch had fallen. No. Been tackled. Taken out of the saddle. There was nothing. No sign of him. He scanned the land around in desperate flashes of the storm now roiling overhead.

He reached up and grabbed the cross on his chest and began mumbling a prayer. If there was ever a time for divine protection, it was now. As he tried to find Mitch, the lights of the rest of the crew raced past him. He had no concept of time. It had been minutes since the strike. Since the herd took off in a panic. Since Paulie and Mitch vanished from sight. He watched the day riders fly past him. James yelled something but it was lost in the noise. He saw them race ahead of the bulk of mindless animals. They had already begun to calm. The earlier escape attempt had left them low on energy and hungry. It was coming under control as rapidly as it began. He kept looking for Paulie or Mitch.

Another flash and he heard what sounded like a pained scream. He jerked the reins toward the direction it appeared to come from. He slowed the horse; the stampede was far ahead of him.

Flash.

He felt his horse rear again but kept a viselike grip on the reins and saddle horn. For a brief moment, he saw what he thought was Danny. But he was on his back on the ground with a look of sheer horror burnt onto his face in the split second of light. Faster and faster the lightning danced across the sky. He couldn't believe his eyes. Danny lay staring up into the storm. A gray skinned human was kneeling in front of him. Spools of ropey intestines lay strewn across the ground. Chris was sure he was hallucinating. There was no way he had seen what he thought. A trick of the storm, he thought. Then another series of rapid-fire bolts. Danny was still lying there. Alone. But his guts were torn out of his now hollow torso. There was no sign of the creature. Or Paulie. Or Mitch. He quickly pulled his shotgun from the holster on the side of his saddle.

He slid down from the saddle and called out softly, "Danny. Can you hear me, man?"

Of course he couldn't. He knelt down and relit his lantern, the winds finally dying down again. He examined the ground and found markings consistent with the thing that had been tearing Danny apart. His blood went cold. He had not imagined it at all. There was something out here with them. He stayed still and listened intently for any sign of the creature. He shined his light toward the tall prairie grass that wasn't trampled down. He felt eyes on him from the large thatch. A low groan carried faintly on the wind.

"Hello? Who's there? Paulie? Mitch?"

There was no answer. The wind picked up and that smell of rot swirled from the swaying grass. He felt himself begin to gag. He took a shaking step forward and used the barrel of his shotgun to part the grass. He was not prepared for what he saw lying in the grass. Paulie lay with his hand over his throat, blood pouring around his fingers. He saw Chris and reached out for him. His entire throat had been torn out. Choking gurgles escaped the ragged hole where his windpipe had been. Chris watched helplessly as his body shook one last time and his arm fell limp. Beneath him was the mangled body of Mitch. His body was crushed by the stampede but there were other marks across his chest. Long slashes that seemed to be caused by . . . fingers from the look of them. But unnaturally sharp. No human could have done that.

The smell didn't fade and he heard the grass move to his side. He could still feel eyes on him as he turned quickly. A sound from in front of him floated to his ears.

"Pleeease . . . "

"Who's there?" he asked. The sound of fear evident to his own ears.

The grass shook and he tried to follow it. Whatever it was moved faster than it should be able to. He whipped his light between the tufts but couldn't catch a view of what it was. It made a full circle around him. It was taunting him.

"Come out here. Face me like a man!" he shouted in rage and frustration.

" . . . don't"

"Don't what? Who are you? What are you?"

"Pleeease . . . "

He heard steps directly behind him and turned and squeezed the trigger. An explosion and flame left the barrels of the shotgun. Too late he saw the shocked expression on Jarod's face as the two handfuls of shot took him in the chest. Chris dropped his weapon and fell to his knees cradling Jarod as he took wet, rasping breaths. Blood welled up and out of his tattered, red and white checkered shirt. He tried to speak but all that came out was a bubble of blood in the lantern light.

James and the remaining four riders found him holding onto Jarod's lifeless body. The scene of carnage in the grass. Danny's half mauled body lying in a pool of blood and dirt. In the distance, the lightning played across the sky as three wolves howled at the nearly invisible moon.

7

CHISHOLM TRAIL

"**AIN'T NO SIGN** of whatever it was that Chris saw. I searched for a mile in all directions." Chad looked at the ground, the images from last night still burnt into his mind.

Chris sat with dark bags around his vacant eyes. He just stared at the fresh patches of dirt with four pairs of empty boots beside them. His hand was rubbing the cross at his throat. Haunted was an apt description for him. James sat not too far away with a mug of coffee sending heat waves into the air in front of him. The heat already felt oppressive as it pulsed down onto the five exhausted survivors.

"I am trying to figure out the math on this one. Five of us. Four, since Jesse has to take the wagon. The remuda is a one-man job alone. That leaves three. How are three of us supposed to successfully guide this many head of cattle all the way to Abilene?" Thomas asked.

James shifted a bit and sipped at the thick black coffee. "All we need is to make it to Duncan. We can get a couple locals to ride with us. We give them Daniel's cut of the pay and a portion of the ones we lost. The rest of the dead men's money goes to their families. It's the only way I can figure. Three days to Duncan. Four if we take it nice and slow. We rest for a week. Then the final push to Abilene."

Thomas looked at him doubtfully but nodded. Chad never looked up from his boots but nodded as well. Jesse didn't care. He had loaded up his stuff and sat next to James with a mug of coffee as well.

Chris stopped twitching. "It was the devil himself."

"It was the storm and a heap of bad luck. The night does things to a man. Plays tricks on him. I reckon the lightning caused the stampede. Danny was crushed nearly immediately. Paulie and Mitch got caught up on it too. It was a freak storm from outta nowhere."

"And the bite marks? Danny was half eaten! Mitch had those claw marks across his face and chest. Paulie too! No stampede of grass eaters did that!" Chris looked feverish as he spoke louder and louder.

Jesse made a face at James, who nodded. He stood and went to the wagon.

"Wolves," Chad said quietly.

James nodded. "We heard enough of the bastards. They must have slinked in under the cover of the storm. Ate their fill of the boys after they got trampled."

"Seems as likely as a monster crept in," Thomas added, not looking toward Chris as he did.

"I know what I saw. There was a creature out there."

"Or you jumped at shadows. Maybe it was Jarod checking on the fallen. James said it. Your mind played tricks on you. You got so worked up from fear and then . . ."

Chris finally got more fire into his eyes. "Then what? What? You think Jarod won't be a ghost floating around my heart until the end of days? It was an accident. Or it wasn't. I don't know. Christ on his cross, I wish I did. I think the creature in the grass baited me into doing it. I think it knew what it was doing and saw a chance to thin our numbers by one more. It is the devil out there, the stench of death hovering over its evil form."

Silence hung over the camp. For a long moment, there was an uneasy feeling as the world itself felt at peace. Nothing stirred.

A hawk circled high above, floating lazily on a thermal as it watched the ground. Its long brown feathers perfectly caught the invisible currents. Sharp black eyes scoured the ground below for any telltale signs of prey on the hardscrabble earth so far underneath. The hawk's head snapped to the side. In an instant, the wings pulled in tightly to its body, like a bullet speeding toward the flash of shadowy movement, its sharp talons and beak at the ready to snatch the morsel in midstep, to tear it to shreds to be eaten.

The hawk's cry pierced the silence at the same time a different cry came bellowing from the back of the wagon. James burst to his feet, with Chad and Thomas right behind him. Chris stared as the wagon began shaking as if in an earthquake. The cross held so tightly in his hands four drops of blood ran down his forearms.

"Jesse! Are you alright in there?" James yelled.

Chris watched in horror as the men circled behind the wagon with guns raised. He heard the exclamations of fear, wordless shouts and gasps. Unintelligible. Gunfire filled the former silence as all three men let loose with the steel in their trembling hands. "Cannot kill the devil," he murmured silently, a tinge of insanity in his hoarse voice. He felt the longhorns panic and begin to scatter to the four winds. It didn't matter. Nothing mattered.

Gray arms reached out and yanked Chad into the wagon as James and Thomas tried to snap speedloaders into place. Chad cried out in terror and pain. Chris watched red liquid ooze down from the slats that made up the floor of the wagon. He watched it hit the ground in fat drops. Then James and Thomas unloaded again. Black seemed to drip with the crimson, thicker, more viscous than the red. Burnt powder filled the air. Then, as the plumes of gun smoke wafted like clouds into the clear azure nothing above, silence fell again.

James turned his head and began vomiting. Thomas just stared without comprehending what was in front of him. Chris watched the red begin to flow faster, like a waterfall. Globs of the black tar fell into the growing puddle. James wretched until his stomach was empty. Then he continued to dry heave.

Thomas turned to Chris. His face was pale from the horror he had just seen. The ghost of a smile turned up the corners of his drooping mustachioed mouth. "We got the bastard. The devil is dead. Damn thing must have snuck into the wagon after breakfast. It's over."

He clapped James on the back and dropped to his knees. Chris watched with tears streaming down his face. The devil was dead. Nine men lost. The entire herd gone. But the devil was dead. Hallelujah. The devil was dead.

A creaking sound came as the wagon shifted a little. James raised his head at the noise. He didn't have time to scream, though. The twisted gray creature launched itself from the wagon and had its jaws, stretched impossibly wide, around James's throat. A wet tearing sound erupted as it wrenched its head back, sending a shower of viscera onto the air. Its head went back again and again, each time spraying more hot blood across the ground. An unearthly howl rumbled out of its mouth that echoed across the flat ground.

Thomas turned to watch, frozen for a moment. Then he turned to Chris and screamed, "Run!!" Chris just sat there, willing his arms and legs to move. But they were still, as if carved from stone.

With an almost casual flick of the too-long claws coming from the gore covered hands, it turned and lopped Thomas's head off. It was so smooth and effortless. It stood with a satisfied grin as the blood fountained up, bathing it until the pressure dropped and the body slumped forward. It cocked its head like a crow and studied Chris as he sat in his urine. It raised one hand and flicked its claws towards him. He watched flecks of blood and skin arc through the air only to fall short of where he sat. The grin turned into a smile devoid of any happiness, a frozen monstrosity that parodied the real thing.

Then it opened its mouth and called out. *"Runnnnnnnnn!"*

That snapped Chris out of the sheer terror that had held him like chains. He leapt to unsteady feet and raced off into the flat lands, not even considering trying to get on one of the horses tied far off to the side. The only thought racing through his mind was to run as fast and as far as possible away from the Devil. He ignored his soaked pants, didn't even feel the cross still jammed into his palm or the leather straps slapping his wrist. He just ran.

And the creature watched. Its nostrils flared as it took in the scent of prey, turning into a blurry spot in the distance. A long tongue jutted out to taste the air as well. The gray skin hung in strips where the bullets had torn through it. The onyx fluid slowly ran across the blood-soaked torso. The all black eyes still followed Chris who was no longer visible.

"Pleeease . . . runnnnnnnnn . . . "

It let out a cruel cackle and then fell onto Thomas's still warm body. The bullets fell to the ground with wet plops as it feasted. A model of efficiency, tearing and ripping through flesh and bone. Perched high above to the South, the hawk tore pieces of the rabbit off and shook them down its throat in a similar act. Chunks of fur lined the bottom of its nest where three eggs lay warmed from the sun.

All the while, Chris just ran.

8

DUNCAN, MORNING

KENZIE STOOD OUTSIDE of the largest building in town and stared up at the lettering painted in bold red across the light gray wood. She watched her bartender and silent partner, Bradley, apply a fresh coat of paint.

"How's this look?" he called down.

She scrunched her face up. "It does look like blood, doesn't it?"

Brad glowered back. "I told you it did before you sent me up here to repaint. I said it looks like blood and asked if that is what you wanted the first image of the business to be. The last color was fine, but no. Mackenzie wants something done."

"You finished?"

He shrugged and went back to painting. The letters were huge, visible nearly before the tall steeple of the church, spelling her name in bright red letters. Would have been even bigger if Josiah hadn't complained that a brothel shouldn't have better line

64

of sight than a church. She didn't care for his logic one bit. But she acquiesced as her daddy had taught her to do, painted on a big smile of agreement, and only allowed Bradley to serve the preacher from the watered-down stock at a slight increase in price.

Kenzie didn't lose. You may not be aware she was winning. But rest assured, by her tally, she came out ahead. She owned the bar, the brothel, and the hotel. Everyone in town gave her a portion of their money. She had wanted to be a writer. By all accounts, she was damn talented at it. But the boys' club back East didn't take to women climbing the ranks. So she spat in the dirt by their polished leather shoes and took her inheritance and moved away. She hated it. She grew up all over the place but had settled in Florida.

Now she was in the middle of nowhere, writing stories in a town of near-illiterates that would never appreciate her genius. One day, she would earn enough to own the whole town. She imagined it growing into a bustling community. She wanted to start a newspaper. Tell the world the truth about the not so wild west. Expose the strong women that fight alongside their husbands. Maybe use the press to put out a few of her own stories. It was just a matter of biding her time.

"I could mix in some white. Make it pink instead," Bradley hollered.

"No. It's fine. I'll get with Tracey and see if we can't get a different shade next time. Maybe a lavender or lilac. Hurry up, now. It's nearly time to open. The guests will be awake soon."

They made a sour face at each other as Bradley did one last coat of paint on the Z. Late last night, a stagecoach had rolled into town. A group of sightseers on their way to California. Fools, every last one of them. Seeking to pan for gold and make their fortunes at the ass edge of America. Too cheap or stupid to take the train. Dazzled by the stories of the lawless West, they hoped to cut down the Chisholm Trail and venture across Texas through the untamed Native lands. The two couples riding in the coach were alright for city slickers from New York. They seemed taken aback by the brothel and bar being attached to the hotel itself. The idea of one stop for all their needs must have been foreign in the big cities.

They weren't the main cause of concern, though. It was the last that rode in beside the coach that gave them both a shiver of worry. Mary Jo was her name. Rumors and tall tales had been floating around the last couple years about her. Foul mouthed and ready for a fight wherever she showed up. As dangerous with her tongue as she was with the pistols that hung on her belt. A painter of some renown that had run afoul of the sheriff of Abilene, the known drunkard and gambler 'Wild Bill' Hickok. Kenzie had heard the tale from some of the cattle drivers on their way back to Texas. Mary Jo was very drunk and wearing nothing but her birthday suit while attempting paint a self portrait on the hotel room wall. Hickok was heard saying as she fled town that he had fought two bears in his life and would gladly fight a third rather than tangle with her again.

And now, she had stumbled into Duncan. The Good Lord himself only knew what kind of trouble she would bring with her.

"We need to only sell her the special batch."

Kenzie stared into space as she spoke. "And hide the rest of that paint when you finish. No need to give her ideas."

Bradley grunted. And climbed down the rickety wooden ladder. "She didn't seem all that bad to me. In fact, she was rather pleasant. I think she may have been a little sweet on me."

Kenzie laughed and stomped her foot on dusty ground. "Ain't no way she found your goofy smile something to be sweet over. And that soup strainer on your lip there. You look like one of those police dogs from up North. What are they called again?"

"A schnauzer. Regal dogs."

She slapped her thigh and tears rolled down her cheeks. "You got it! A schnauzer! You look as regal as a one dicked weasel!"

"For someone so fancy with words, you are spiteful and uncultured sometimes, Kenzie. Hurtful, too."

"Awww. Don't you fret none, Bradley. I'll get you one of the soup bones to gnaw on until your naked outlaw comes down to paint your portrait. Maybe she'll scratch behind your ears as well."

He tried to glare at her but the twinkle in his eyes gave him away. "I do believe you are jealous, Ms. Kenzie. Afraid she will sweep me off my feet and take me out of this two-horse town?"

"I will gladly give her both of the horses if she does."

"And then who would serve drinks to the patrons of your fine establishment?"

"Marie. Tara. Tina. The mule out by the Indians. Lana. Bella. Amber. Teddy."

"Now hold your horses one second. Teddy is a known drunk and thief."

"That's why he was my last choice."

"And the mule being before most of the girls?"

"That is just logical."

"Maybe you're a little right on that. I'll send you a letter once we settle into our chateau. Somewhere by the water. I can bury my toes in the sand and watch the waves."

Kenzie gave him a serious look. "You may be drifting a little too far into the fairy tale."

He grinned his lopsided grin at her. "See? I knew you couldn't bare the idea of being without me."

She clapped him on the back and laughed. "C'mon in. We got to get the ladies up. Our guests will be down and expecting breakfast, I imagine."

Bradley stopped and looked up at the fresh paint. He grimaced as he saw the cheap red was running a bit down the wood. It really did look like blood, he thought to himself. A crow cawed and sent a chill down his spine. He wasn't a religious man, nor superstitious. But he made the sign of the cross, anyway. Just to be safe. Then he followed Kenzie in and got himself resigned to making eggs and bacon for the five guests and the wagon driver. And the girls would expect something as well. He sighed with contentment. After so long traveling from place to place, it was nice to have somewhere to call home. And maybe if he played his cards right, an outlaw artist to spend a few hours with in private.

HUNGER ON THE CHISHOLM TRAIL

Tracey woke with a start and grabbed the gun off of the bedside table. She pulled back the hammer and waved it slowly around the room. Her eyes were slits as she warily searched the shadows. A dream. It was just a dream, she told herself before easing the hammer back. Another nightmare. She felt the layer of sweat that coated her body under the sleep dress. As much a sign of the nightmare as the oppressive heat that already permeated the small attic room above her shop. Her Shop. The thought of it was nearly enough to erase the dream from her mind. It was all hers. Bought and paid for her with the money left to her by her parents she had managed to hide away before making her escape across the ocean.

Her mind went back to home for a moment. The gray skies over the churning waves. Orchids filling the air. The chilly wind carrying the taste of salt throughout her room. She missed it sometimes. Until thoughts of Him intruded. His drunken rage, the smell of cheap liquor and whore perfume clinging to his clothes as he bellowed for dinner. His heavy hands as he raised them in anger.

No. This was home. Far from everything she knew and loved. Far from the man she hated enough to disappear into the trail dust and sweat of nowhere. But that didn't stop the dreams. Didn't stop the terror of the last night in her childhood home. The sound of glass shattering. Of fine China in ruins as the thickly pooling blood came closer and closer to where she stood.

She shook her head to clear the thoughts, saw the glass on the table and reached for it. It sat peacefully, with little swirls of the thicker solution catching the

69

light as it came through the small window above her bed. The promise of nothing lay in that glass. Yet, she stopped herself. It was too early for numbing. Even if the urge was too strong. The temptation calling from her every cell to just take a sip and let the past slide into shadows beneath her bed. She couldn't. The store had to be tidied, even though no one had come for the last couple days. Except the Sheriff and Mr. Beck.

He was a curious one. She had heard the rumors. Everyone had. Arrested for trying to conjure demons at Kenzie's his first night in town. A scholar of some sort, traveling around in search of mystery.

And handsome.

Not classically handsome, but appealing. She caught herself thinking of him in such a way and blushed. He would be gone soon, and she would still be here. No time for silly fantasy. The cattle drives would be here soon. She could forget her past, stop daydreaming and focus on the present. That's all that mattered. The here and now. She was unaware she had picked up the glass and taken a long drink until she tasted the sourness of the Laudanum as it hit her tongue. She felt disappointed in herself for a moment. A brief moment. Then she shrugged and drained the rest of the glass. No sense in wasting it.

It took a few moments for the feeling of abandon to travel down her legs, to ease the tension she was not aware of in her back and neck. But once it did, she found herself floating on a cloud. Sure, it made thinking harder, but it made remembering near impossible. That was enough for her as she slowly made her way down the stairs to her shop. She raised the blind on the door and caught a view of Mr. Beck,

Karl, sitting alone in the sheriff's office. She watched him sip coffee and shuffle through the books spread out in front of him. He was curious, wearing a nice suit with his bald head catching the light. He looked up and waved at her and she nearly jumped. She had lost track of time in her musing. She sheepishly raised a hand back and then scurried away. Her face was nearly the same shade as the fresh paint dripping slowly down the front of the bar.

She froze at the back of the store, remembering the dinner this evening at Mikhail and Jia-Li's home. She could just beg off due to a headache. The entire town knew about her headaches, after all. But she let herself imagine sitting around the table. Laughing with the others as they told tales of time before Duncan. Perhaps Karl would walk her home. A kiss upon her hand for having shared the evening.

She laughed at herself.

No. She would decline this evening's festivities. But she grabbed the finest bottle of whiskey off of the shelf for them. She took a knife and marred the label slightly. Just enough. She could tell him it was free due to damage. She smiled at that. She may not be there physically, but she could be there in spirit. Or spirits, as the case may be.

Even as she smiled, a flash of sorrow swept through her eyes. She blinked it away. Dreams were just that. Silly things. She had a business to run. If she desired the company of a man so badly, well, she could take one of the riders upstairs when the herds started pouring into town. No strings attached to one of those free roaming idiots. No curiosity, either. Just a few moments of sweat filled action.

Josiah knelt on the hardwood before the cross on the back wall of the church. His fevered words drifted softly through the large room.

"Father, grant me the strength to stay away from the bottle. The courage to face my demons and stand tall as they claw in my belly. I am weak, but steadfast in your teachings. I shall play your words upon the flock, tending to their spiritual distress and guiding them toward the promise of heaven. Amen."

He rose slowly, his knees not what they had been in his youth. He could feel the scar where the arrow had pierced his leg throb as he stood. One of many pains caused by the red skinned bastards. He knew it was wrong to be filled with hatred. That it went against the gospels. But try as he may, the memories of good Christians being slaughtered by the heathens tore through his mind. He would gladly have gone back to Illinois after the fighting. Returned to his family and friends. But he felt the call of the Lord draw him to Duncan. Perhaps it was also due to the shame he felt. It was not just his knee that had been injured in the fighting. But his soul, as well. He had done, seen, been party to and turned a blind eye from atrocities. He told himself what had been done had been for the greater glory. But the drink called as well. And when he fell into the cups, he wondered if it all hadn't been one big lie.

He felt shame burn through him. Heard the whispers of doubt. The urge to fall back to his knees and seek forgiveness like waves of the sea splashed through him. But the ache in his knees screamed just as loud. He limped toward the doorway. He saw Bradley climb down from the ladder. Saw the blood red paint on the whorehouse mocking him. He would go there and give them a piece of his mind. Drawing more attention to the depravities of man in a town that should stand as a beacon. It was disgusting. And maybe a slug or two of whiskey. No more. Just enough to ease the ache.

Teddy woke in a panic. The world was dark, yet he heard the chickens and roosters raising a fuss somewhere. He sat up and felt an intense pain as his head hit something hard. Coupled with the nausea of his insides feeling like they were liquefied from too much rot gut, the sudden hammering of nails into his skull was more than he could handle. He rolled to his side and vomited bile and acid onto the hay covered floor. When the purge ended, he rolled carefully back on to his back and stared up in sick confusion.

Slowly, the world regained definition as his guts rolled. He was in the barn out behind the hotel. Blurry images of stumbling from the bar. No. Being tossed out of the bar by Bradley at Kenzie's behest. Staggering into the barn and seeing the stagecoach parked inside. He had rifled through it, but anything of value must have gone inside with the guests. The lockbox on the back had been secured from ne'er-do-wells such as himself. He tried to sleep on the cushions inside the coach but was unable to get comfortable on the threadbare seats. He recalled stepping. No. Falling out of the coach and rolling underneath to avoid being caught by Bradley or one of the girls.

He had his pride still, what little remained. He'd been run out of better towns than this. But those had been a day or two of stumbling apart. He had barely made it from Kansas to this pockmark on the backside of the civilized world. Did the odd job for the farmers or around town. Usually just enough to earn enough rot gut to stop the shaking in his hands. His poor, worn out hands. He raised them up and stared at them. They had built great buildings. He had been in construction for years until the influenza had come to town. The last bit of good work they did was digging holes in the ground to lay his sweet Emma and Gertrude into.

Now they shoveled shit in the stables. And were happy to do so. How far had he sunk? Spending his days near-sick with need for a drink. His evenings making up for lost time. All the while thinking of those better days. Josiah said it was them Injuns that sent the flu. Said it was payback for the Trail of Tears. Teddy didn't agree with that. Not really. But Josiah would buy as long as he listened and didn't argue. Only a fool could say no to free drinks. So what if Josiah was a bit off with his ramblings? His coin spent like any other. And no one else wanted to listen to him. It was very nearly a friendship. Close. Drinking partners.

Good enough for him. Even if them uppity whores didn't like it. Who were they, anyway? Spending the summer and fall on their backs with their legs spread for the cattlemen. None of them ever worked a day in their lives. They didn't understand loss.

Josiah did, though. Maybe he was done praying and would need a drink soon. It was a few days until the cattle came. Then he would have work to do. Taking care of the horses. Helping Tracey unload her deliveries. Maybe this season he could save up enough to get to the train. Buy a ticket to the coast. Either. He didn't really care. He nodded. He would. He'd get himself dried out on the train ride. Start fresh in whatever city he got let out in. Maybe go back to construction. Just a few more months. That was all.

He rolled out from under the coach and carefully opened the door to the barn. Everyone was probably eating breakfast. He crept out to the street where he saw Josiah leaving the church with a pained limp. He couldn't help but smile. The only thing that helped his limp was whiskey. It'd be a damned shame to make the man drink alone.

Cody walked down the empty main street of town, a smile on his face as he looked at the quiet world around him. He would one day have his own practice in a thriving town, he thought to himself. One of these days. The rest of the world was not ready for his particular ideas. He sat at the cutting edge of medicine. Unfortunately for him, the cutting edge was frightful to the closed-minded folks. Filled with superstitions and folk tales, they had run him out of more than one town over the years. But he would show them. Science was based on fact, not hoodoo and the such. He experimented to further that science. And a town like Duncan was the perfect place for that. Out of view of the peering eyes of the ignorant masses.

He reached into his pocket and pulled out his latest find. A small handful of mushrooms he had gotten from River and Hasse. He had sampled some the night before. Judging by his notes and the way he recalled feeling, these could be the find of the century. He could barely keep the smile from his face. These so-called savages had so many unique cures and ideas. He longed to spend a few days with the medicine man of the tribes, but River refused to even entertain the idea. The cold science went too far against their spiritual beliefs in the common thread of nature. He had tried to convince River that they were both the same. It was the understanding of the science that lay beneath the spiritual he sought.

The mushrooms were his test. To see if he could reach his spirituality. He believed that he had. And he longed to try again. But they came with the words that ingesting too many too often reduced the strength. He theorized it built up an immunity against the powerful hallucinogenic effect. They had awoken something within him last night, though. That much was certain. What other wonders did the tribes know of that could benefit all of mankind?

He passed the store and waved to Tracey with a grin. She smiled and waved back. He turned and saw Karl in the sheriff's office and tipped his hat to him and received a warm smile and nod. Then he straightened up a bit as he saw Josiah limp out of the church. The two of them did not see eye to eye very often, but both brought their own value to Duncan. Though Cody failed to understand exactly what it was

Josiah brought. There was no need of God in science, none he could find in any relation. But there was something to faith that seemed to accelerate the process of healing. It was a quandary that would require a better preacher than Josiah to answer. He opened his mouth to give a greeting when Teddy stumbled out from behind the brothel. He smiled, saved by the oaf racing towards the preacher. Drinking partners meeting up to begin another day of debauchery. He was not even noticed as he passed them. More the better. Though he wondered at what the mushrooms would do for one so far into the bottle as Teddy. Could they be used to wean him off of the drink? A curious idea.

He passed the post office that also served as the bank and nodded to Robert. Robert was a stern man that barely spoke. He sat in the post office, more a glorified shed, from sunrise to sundown. He didn't socialize much. A teetotaler. Attended church on Sundays and then returned to either his office or his home behind it. There was not much call for either bank or post office with such a small population but, once the government gave the okay for settlers to rush in, there would be. It was just a matter of time. Duncan was one of the first of the settlements, the Sooner movement as they called themselves, and the others spread across the region. On the rare occasions he got to talking, all Robert could speak of was the day when he would get his first telegraph rig. He was obsessed with the multiline telegraph system and assured everyone it would soon come to Duncan. Robert nodded curtly back to Cody as he walked.

Smoke rose into the sky in front him as he

approached the toll collection hut. It was smaller than any building in town and clearly constructed by Natives. As he approached, Hasse leaned out the opening and smiled at him. He grinned back and hurried his steps. Hasse held the buffalo hide open for him and he ducked in. His eyes burned from the small fire in the center of the room. River sat cross legged on the floor and grunted at Cody.

"Good morning, gentlemen."

"Sawbones. I see you survived your journey last night."

"A miraculous one at that! These mushrooms of yours could hide great medicinal properties. I was hoping to get more of them as soon as possible."

Hasse gestured to River who nodded. "We can help you with that. How are things in town? A coach came in late with a rider following."

Cody nodded and sat down, mimicking the cross-legged position. "Travelers headed to California. And an artist, I believe."

Hasse gestured again. River watched and gestured back. They went back and forth for a few minutes before Hasse threw up his arms and stomped out.

"Why doesn't he ever speak? I see no scarring."

River shrugged.

"You don't know? Or you won't say?"

River cocked his head at him. "I see no difference. What concern is it of yours?"

"Curiosity, mostly. I could help him."

"None can help him. He has taken a vow."

"A vow?"

"Yes. The last word he uttered was of a great evil loosed upon the world. He has sworn to end it."

"What kind of evil?"

River looked into the fire. "I don't know. Three years ago, I found him. He was near death. I took him back to the tribes. He has not spoken a word. The medicine man spoke with the spirits. Coyote revealed himself. He has two paths in front of him. One of great good. Or one of great evil. But they are his alone to choose."

"You're some strange folk."

River smiled and nodded.

9

DUNCAN, NIGHT FALLING

KARL STOOD LOOKING at himself in the small shaving mirror. He didn't like the face looking back at him. "When did I get so old? A week ago, I was in Paris, drinking wine and celebrating the beheading of the vampire in the catacombs. Now look at yourself. The damnable creature looked better than you do now."

He pulled out his grooming kit and trimmed the wiry gray hairs that seemed to stand no matter how he brushed them. He sighed and put it all away. For all of his adventures, time was the one beast he could not slay. And he was tired. Bone tired. Enough so that staying a week in a small town jail was the best vacation he had in years. No monsters. No violence. Just relaxation, whiskey, good conversation and a nice view. He found himself staring across the street at the shop. He needed to go get the whiskey. But had found himself making excuses not to do it. He found himself rooted with nervousness, he had dealt with the occasional pretty lass over the years. He wasn't afraid of them. But days of secret looks across the street had made him a mess.

He blamed Mikhail for trying to act like a matchmaker. Damned fool sheriff. What did he gain from it? He was leaving for the West Coast as soon as he was relieved of duty. And he blamed himself for standing there staring like an idiot. He had faced things that would most likely melt the mind of the average man. And now a good-looking dame with sad eyes had him all sorts of sixes and sevens.

"You'll get the damned whiskey. If she is so inclined, you will escort her to the sheriff's. No different than stumbling into the den of those ghouls. Or that one time the cultists accidentally awoke the thing that slumbered beneath Boston. Pull yourself together, you fool."

He strode purposefully out the door and walked with his head held high across the street. The door was propped open, so he stepped inside and cleared his throat to announce himself.

"Mr. Beck. I have been expecting you all day." Tracey looked at him with a half smile.

"My pardon for the lateness of my arrival. Lost in thought for the bulk of the day."

She nodded. "I found that bottle of whiskey the sheriff asked you to pick up." She placed it on the counter and he eyed it appreciatively. Then she made a face of despair. "Oh no."

He looked startled and unconsciously his hand went to the pistol on his left side as he turned quickly.

She laughed at him and then pointed. "The damned thing is damaged. Must have happened in the shipping. I cannot, in good conscience, charge you for this bottle. Please accept it with deepest condolences." Her words were a little thick but there was a gleam in her eyes he appreciated.

"And will you do me the honor of joining for the night's festivities? I hate to ask, but I am a stranger in this strange land. It would do my heart good to have a friend in my corner."

She stared at him. "I would love to, but . . . "

He didn't allow her to finish the inevitable excuse he saw her mind trying to spin. She clearly needed to get out of this small building. Fresh air and conversation would do her good. "Fantastic. Let me help you lock up and we can be on our way!"

Her mouth opened and closed a few times. She didn't quite know what to do or say. "But . . . "

"No, ma'am, I insist on helping. Two sets of hands are better than one. Besides, it is getting close to fashionable late. I'd hate to be a poor guest."

She just nodded at him, a blush creeping up her cheeks. Before she knew what was happening, she was locking the door to the shop and accepting his arm for the stroll to the sheriff's house. Her mind swam with the Laudanum and anxiety. She wanted to run back inside and slam the door. To hide in her bed. Instead, she found herself resting her hand on his arm.

"I am a little nervous, if I am being honest with you. I've not spent much time around people from the Orient. I feel less than confident in my knowledge of proper etiquette."

Tracey nodded. "Jia-Li is quite polite, Mr. Beck. I don't think you will have much to concern yourself with. Mikhail isn't the most gentile man in town, yet they seem to be pretty happy."

"That is true. Thank you for setting my mind at ease. Now, how about telling me about yourself? I'll admit to no small measure of curiosity."

"Not much to tell. Grew up in a small town to the East of London, near the sea. My parents passed away and I made my way to Duncan. I miss the ocean. And the rains. Not much else, though." Her eyes grew far away and her grip on his arm tightened slightly as she went far away.

"Pardon my forwardness, but how did such a handsome woman as yourself manage to avoid marriage?"

She laughed lightly, a lovely sound to Karl's ears. "I didn't avoid it. It just wasn't the life for me, I found." Her smile faltered as she spoke. "He passed. I suddenly found myself with no family, a widow and no desire to remain. I took the first ship I could to the New World."

Karl nodded thoughtfully. "My sincerest apologies for dredging up the past. My mouth tends to move faster than my sense."

She didn't answer for a long moment, so they walked on in silence.

"Well ain't you two just so sweet on an evening stroll?" a voice called from the shadows on the side of the road. The shadow stepped forward onto the street, revealing herself.

"Good evening to you, madam," Karl answered. He felt Tracey stiffen next to him and patted her arm gently to let her know it was alright. "I'm guessing you came with the stagecoach last night?"

The woman, dressed in leathers with a checkered shirt cut in a man's style turned her head and spat into the dust. "Reckon I came in alongside them no good coffee boilers. But I ain't with them one bit. My da always told me them city folk from back East is crooked as a Virginia fence. And me? I may have been accused a bein' a chucklehead once or twice, but I ain't one of them lily livered chickenshits. No, sir."

"And what, pray tell, are you exactly, madam?" Tracey asked, surprised at the language this lady so casually spoke. Even the cattlemen spoke with more aplomb when they came to town.

"Well, hell. I ain't no madam, that's fer damn sure. Me? I fancy myself an artist. Due to a slight misunderstanding between me and ole Wild Bill back in Abilene, I find myself a bit of an outlaw as well."

"An artist, you say? What is your preferred medium, if I might inquire? And your name, as well?" Karl asked politely.

"Shit and tarnation. Ain't you both cultured sumbitches? Mary Jo is the name my da gave me. Only God damned thing he ever did give me at that, 'sides a kick in the ass when I turned eighteen. I like to paint if'n I'm given the chance. Gonna head out toward California way, maybe up to Oregon. First things first, I'm gonna get the handsome bartender into my bed. Maybe paint his picture, if you catch my drift."

Tracey blushed and Karl let out a belly laugh. "Well then, Mary Jo, I wish you good luck. Both on your trip and with the bartender."

She spat onto the ground again and smiled. "Same to the two of you love birds. Good evening. Time to catch myself that greased hog." She tipped her hat and began walking back towards the bar.

"She seems quite colorful," Karl whispered.

"Seems to be trouble." Tracey turned her head to watch as Mary Jo walked down the street. "Precisely the type of person we do not need in Duncan."

Karl laughed. "It takes all sorts to make this world turn. Though I may feel sorry for Bradley in the morning if she gets her way."

"This is the sheriff's house," Tracey pointed to a nice little house tucked just off of the main street.

Karl held open the gate on the fence and Tracey curtseyed a bit wobbly as she passed. He pulled it carefully shut as she knocked on the door. Mikhail answered looking dapper in what Karl assumed were his church clothes. "Karl! And Tracey! You look lovely as always. Please come in." He turned and spoke loudly, "Jia, my love, our guests have arrived."

Karl didn't know what to expect. His few interactions with the Chinese were mostly spent in seedier locations in New York and on occasion in San Francisco. He had once tracked a Fae into an opium den in Chicago in the rundown Chinatown area. He didn't tend to lump all of a people together based on a small sample, so he kept his mind open for anything.

But when Jia-Li came from the back room, his breath was taken away. To say she was beautiful was akin to saying the sunrise was pleasant as it rose over the ocean and painted the waves like diamonds. She was petite, especially compared to her husband who stood roughly six foot tall. Where he was weathered from years of riding in the sun, she was flawless like fine porcelain, but with a natural tan complexion.

He didn't realize his jaw had dropped until

Mikhail laughed and clapped him on the shoulder. "I made the same face when I first saw her. My Jewel of the Orient."

Jia-Li laughed and Karl couldn't help but laugh as well through his blush. "A pleasure to make your acquaintance, Mr. Beck. Mikhail has told me all about you," she said in perfect English. "And Tracey! I'm so happy you came. I feared it would be an evening of the men telling half truths while I nodded and pretended to believe them."

Karl's jaw dropped open again.

"Thank you, ma'am. The pleasure is all mine." Tracey kissed Jia-Li on the cheek as Karl handed the bottle of whiskey to Mikhail. Jia-Li and Tracey went back into the kitchen as Mikhail grabbed a couple glasses off of a shelf and cracked open the whiskey.

"How in the hell did you manage to trick her into marrying you?"

Mikhail laughed as he poured. "If I had a nickel for every time someone asked me that, I could retire."

Karl took the glass. "We met a stranger on the way over just now."

"The outlaw? Mary Jo, the nude painter. I stopped in to make sure she wasn't going to be causing any trouble earlier."

"She is a character."

"So you managed to finagle the shopkeeper out. How'd you do that?"

Karl shrugged. "Just asked nicely. And then didn't give her a choice in the matter."

"Why Mr. Beck, you strong-armed the poor woman."

"In a polite way. Yes. She seemed to be in dire need of a night out."

"I reckon you are correct in that. Come and relax. I'm sure supper is very nearly finished."

As if reading the future, Jia-Li and Tracey stepped out with full trays and began placing them on the table. The room filled with the scent of rosemary and sage. Mikhail began serving out the meal as Karl sat and sipped at his glass. Karl offered the ladies whiskey, but both declined, even if Tracey had an expression of desire for a tall glass. She settled for a red wine, the color of blood, same as Jia-Li. Karl stared appreciatively at the meal.

"Is this a ratatouille?" he asked, his stomach rumbling.

Jia-Li smiled. "Yes it is. You have dined on French cuisine before?"

"Spent a fair amount of time in France over the years. Most recently I was in New Orleans, as well. Not the same, but close enough for my untrained palate. You?"

She shook her head. "No, though I dream of it one day. I worked in a restaurant in Chicago for a few years before Mikhail lured me in with the promise of San Francisco. What's wrong, you appear surprised."

Mikhail burst out laughing at the expression on Karl's face. Jia-Li and Tracey looked at him in surprise for a moment before going in themselves.

"What was it this time? Did he say he found me working in an opium den? Or was it the one where he rescued me from slavers?" she asked.

"Umm. He said you were with your father building railroads."

She reached over and gently stroked Mikhail's cheek. "Ah. That one. I'm sure he said I didn't speak English at all. That he saved me and taught me to speak correctly before begging my father to marry me."

Tracey drained her glass of wine and enjoyed the discomfort on Karl's face. "That was the one. I barely kept a straight face."

Karl looked at her in feigned offense. "You knew?"

She nodded and blushed in a pretty way. Mikhail slapped his though as laughter rumbled from him. "It's a mite better than the truth."

Jia-Li laughed even harder. "Yes. The policeman that fell in love with the sous chef. Tell him how you came to the restaurant every day. Or how you begged my father for my hand in marriage, darling.

"He said no. Four times. Didn't feel I was good enough for her."

"He finally relented out of pity. He saw how tightly you were wrapped around my finger. He often asked me to test your adoration by having you roll over and beg. My stray puppy, so obedient and in love."

They looked at each other and Karl felt a pang of jealousy at the unbridled love between them. Out of the corner of his eye, he saw Tracey wore the same expression of longing he was sure was on his face. He smiled sadly and took a long drink of the whiskey, savoring the burn as it traveled down his throat. Love was one of many things he had to sacrifice to keep the world safe. Or that was the lie he told himself during the many lonely nights on the road. What did he have to offer anyone, really? Eventually just a corpse when he picked the wrong fight. It was better this way.

HUNGER ON THE CHISHOLM TRAIL

Jia-Li seemed to remember herself and reached over and took Karl's hand. He jumped a little, startled from his reverie. He saw she held Mikhail's hand as well and gestured with her head toward Tracey. He understood after a moment. He reached over and took Tracey's hand and bowed his head as Mikhail said the prayer. He had seen so much over the years, things that made faith fleeting. But he respected faith, knew it could be a powerful thing in the hands of a believer. For good or evil. When she finished, he found himself disappointed when Tracey took her hand back, the residual warmth of it tingling across his own

They did not hesitate after the prayer to begin to eat. Mikhail watched as the guests tore into the food as if they had not eaten in weeks. "She shot the rabbits herself. Not only is she the best cook in town, but likely the best shot as well."

She smiled with pleasure at his words. "Now now, my pup, let them eat in peace. They are quite aware you married far out of your depth with me."

Karl snorted and choked a little at that. "He did indeed, ma'am. This may be the finest meal I have ever partaken of. Thank you for sharing it with a stranger."

She smiled. "So well mannered. I can see why our Ms. Tracey is taken with you."

It was Tracey's turn to choke. Karl felt heat blossom on his cheeks and knew without looking Tracey was feeling the same. They ate in silence for a long while, neither willing to look up from their plates. Soon, Karl was disappointed to see the bone white of the dish reflecting the lantern light. Jia-Li ladled more and gave him a second thick slice of the fresh baked bread.

"Mikhail tells me you hunt monsters and save the world. Is it true?"

Tracey set down her fork and took a sip of wine while watching him from over the rim of her glass. Mikhail ate slowly and watched as well. Karl moved his food around with a chunk of the bread.

"Do you believe him? About the monsters and such?" He took a bite of the bread and chewed patiently.

"I believe you," Tracey said softly. "I've seen them. I know they are real."

"None of us doubt you. Not exactly. But the monsters, they're just people. Right? I've seen them myself. Men with something missing inside. Just born evil. Broken." Mikhail finished his glass and refilled it. He pushed the bottle to Karl, a haunted look in his eyes.

"I think not, my love. A bad man is still just a man. I believe Karl has seen real monsters. The kind that most only see in dream."

Mikhail made a face but didn't argue.

The table grew silent as Karl filled his glass. "You're both right. Some monsters are just men. And, no offense, ladies as well. Some of the greatest atrocities I have witnessed were committed by people. It has been my displeasure to deal with them." He took a drink and let the whiskey burn away the sour taste of bad memories. "But there are things out there that defy common sense. Not all evil, mind you. In my time, though, I fear the majority of them to be. If not exactly evil, then driven by hungers and desires we see as so."

Mikhail laughed for a second, then realized he was alone. "Is this a campfire story, one you tell to scare your friends?"

Karl chuckled. "If only that were the truth."

"So your tall tale about Luck being a treasure needed to save the world?"

"An unfortunate reality. One of many."

Jia-Li held up a hand. "Luck?"

"There are stories, whispers really, that somewhere in the New World there is a treasure hidden. One the Natives helped to keep from the eyes of the conquering Europeans. In the tales I've been told, it is the mastery of Luck itself. One day the Chosen One, or Fool depending on translation, will find it. This will be the only thing that stands against the end of everything."

No one spoke at all. The only sound was them drinking and the wind blowing outside. Karl looked at the plate of food in front of him and longed to dive back in but there was a tension in the room now that stopped him. He supposed it had been too much to think they would talk of normal things. This was his curse. He didn't know normal, couldn't comprehend it.

"I saw a monster. Back in England. I don't know what it was, not really." Tracey looked as shocked as everyone else when she broke the silence.

"Go on, please," Jia-Li beckoned.

She looked at everyone. They all nodded to her. Mikhail refilled her wine and quickly went to fetch a fresh bottle. She sipped it nervously and then visibly steeled herself.

"In Southend-On-Sea, the town I grew up in, I saw

it. Many times, though at first I had no idea that it was a monster straight out of a Penny Dreadful." She saw questioning looks at that. "Penny Dreadfuls were these scary stories. All sorts of terrible things. My mum would read them to me sometimes if I promised her I wouldn't have nightmares. I always promised, even though nine out of ten times I would in fact have nightmares and end up in bed with her. I think she liked it when I crawled into bed with her to be honest. My father was a fisherman and would be gone for days at a time, you see. And she only ever read them to me when he was gone.

"Anyway. Some nights I would stare out the window of my bedroom and watch the moon on the water. It was calming to me. It made me happy to see it dance along so free. Until one evening when I was seven.

"I was watching the waves and felt myself growing sleepy. It was autumn and the air outside was cool and crisp. As I stared out the window my breath fogged up the glass. As I watched the waves through the foggy pane, I saw someone crawl from the water onto the shore. I wiped the glass thinking it was a mistake. No, there was what looked like a man standing on the wet sand. In my young brain, I guessed it was someone out for a moonlit swim regardless of the brisk weather. Then the man, or what I thought was a man turned and looked right into my window. At me. And I felt my bladder release as I saw two eyes of fire lock onto mine. I screamed and ran into my mum's room.

"She didn't believe me. Thought it was another flight of fancy from her little Magpie. But I insisted he was there. She finally gave in and put on her long robe and walked to the beach where I had seen him. I stood by my now open window and yelled directions to her. When she got to where the thing had been, she found no sign. Of course, the waves had swept the footprints away."

"You were tired, clearly your mind played tricks on you. Perhaps the candlelight in your room reflected just right to appear to be eyes," Mikhail said as she took a long drink of wine.

Tracey nodded. "I would have to agree with you. In fact, I did for years. It took me quite a while to look back out the window. Eventually, my love affair with the moon returned. I had explained away the vision as one of a foolish child.

Until a few years later when I saw him again. Now I was ten and less likely prone to hysterics. It was the same as before. A man walked from the water onto the beach and stood staring at the moon. I crouched lower and tried to memorize every detail. This time the moon was full and cast silver light onto the sand. He was tall, far taller than any man I had seen before. With, I don't know how to explain it, growths like scales or plates across his naked form. I crept to the candle and blew it out then went back to the window but he was gone. I didn't bother my mother this time. I ran out of the house and snuck down to the water edge. This time I was in time to see its footprints in the sand. Then I had no real reference, but my time in the New World has broadened my knowledge. The closest thing I have seen to those footprints was the claws of an alligator like in the swamps."

"Did you ever see him again?" Jia-Li asked in a whisper.

Tracey didn't answer for a long time, lost in the memory. Her hand on the stem of the wine glass whitened as she clenched it tightly. Karl reached carefully over and rested his hand on her wrist and she snapped back to the present. Her hand relaxed and she gave him a small smile. "Yes. A few times over the years. I tried to casually ask others if they had ever seen anything strange come out of the waves. No one ever saw the thing with claws and fire red eyes. Or none that would admit it. Nearly every time I saw it was the same. Just for a moment. I would hide when it turned toward my window. I later heard that on the same occasions I saw the monster, sheep would wind up missing from random farms. A mystery none ever managed to solve. Except for me. I knew the truth."

"Now Tracey, you know I have nothing but the utmost respect for you. But that is the biggest cockamamie tale I ever did hear." Mikhail shook his head and smiled. "Ain't there supposed to be leprechauns and such over there with pots of gold?"

Karl cleared his throat and Mikhail gave him a funny look. "First, leprechauns are everywhere. The lands of Faery open to all places. And they have great hoards of gold and gems. Conniving little bastards they are. I met one in New York City ten or fifteen years ago. Scramulous O'Shea was his name. A right little horse's ass.

"Second, what Tracey saw is rather uncommon. They are known as Sahuagan. They usually lurk in the deep waters. Your former home must butt up against traditional hunting grounds of theirs. You're fortunate all it took was sheep. They are rather, umm, indiscriminate eaters."

HUNGER ON THE CHISHOLM TRAIL

Mikhail opened and closed his mouth three or four times and then decided it was best to just take a long drink of his whiskey. It didn't escape anyone at the table's notice when Tracey reached and grabbed Karl's hand. He stiffened for a second and then blushed slightly. Jia-Li and Mikhail smiled faintly but pretended not to see.

"My father, my baba as I call him, told many stories from China. Have you ever read Journey to the West?"

Karl shook his head. "Heard some of the tales. Sun Wukong and the Celestial Peaches stuck out to me. Your family's neck of the world is not one I've ever had the fortune of making it to in all my travels. The things I've heard took hold of my imagination, though."

Jia-Li beamed at hearing this. "There is a common misconception about China. That the people are all poor farmers. Superstitious and fearful. While it is true for a lot of Chinese, there is rich history as well. And many amazing stories. My grandfather told stories of large hairy man-apes that lived on the snowy peaks. They were shy creatures that hid in the snow and ice to avoid people. He would tell us that one day when he was a child, there was an avalanche that swept down the mountain. Many people were killed and injured. He escaped unharmed, thank God. But as he was searching for other survivors, he said he found one of the man-apes pinned beneath a tree. He was very frightened of it but could not bear to see it suffer. So he used a long thick branch to lift the tree. The creature stared at him for a long moment. He swears it smiled at him before rushing off into the woods as other people approached. No one believed him in the village. But I always did. Man cannot hope to know everything in this great big world. Only God knows."

Karl nodded. "I believe they are called Yeti. In the Everglade swamps in Florida there are a tribe of cousins to the Yeti known as Sasquatch. I've heard rumor of another tribe in Oregon and Northern California as well, but have not seen them myself."

Mikhail muttered under his breath in disbelief. Jia-Li patted his hand gently. "Now, my pup, there surely cannot live so much doubt in you. How many tales must you hear, yet still deny? You close your mind to possibilities because they do not fit into your narrow view. Look how different you and I are, yet we fit together perfectly. Like a key into a lock. Let me try and unlock your brain as well as your heart, my love."

"It just isn't right according to the church and bible. Monsters on mountains, under the sea, and leprechauns! If they existed, why doesn't the good book mention them?"

Karl sipped his whiskey. "You may find yourself surprised at what the church does and does not know. They have done their best to keep things from the public eye. Some for their own good, some for yours and some for the creatures as well. There is a delicate balance between our nature and the nature of other realms. Hell, I don't expect you to just take my word for it. I know I sure as shit didn't when it was first explained to me. I just hope you never find yourself in a predicament where your inability to believe hampers common sense. Some creatures are friendly, but foreign. Sone are similar to us, yet alien in thought. The world is a scary and beautiful place. As long as you're careful. And lucky."

"I like campfire tales as much as the next man. But until I have proof, that is all they are. I'm sorry. I'm not calling you liars. You believe what you believe. But I need to be shown to believe." Mikhail looked unapologetic as he sat there.

Karl stood up and slowly removed his jacket and placed it over the chair. Then he unbuttoned his shirt. He managed to look embarrassed as his middle age showed to be catching up to him. The thick thatch of chest hair had gone more silver and the once solid stomach had drifted slightly over his belt. Tracey looked at him with a fire in her eyes, clearly enjoying the show. His torso was lined with pale marks. Knives, bullets, and what looked like acid splashings mottled his skin.

"Now wait just a second, Karl. You're bordering on the disrespectful here."

Jia-Li grabbed his forearm and he stopped talking as Karl turned around and let them look at his back. It was crossed with deep scarring, thick puckered lines and sunken, missing chunks. Mikhail let out a low whistle. But what stood out was claw marks, deep rents in the flesh that could have been easily mistaken for a bear attack. If a bear had eight distinct claws that resembled misshapen human hands. The sixteen lines, two sets, ran down from his shoulders to right above his belt and ended in distinct palm marks. There could be no doubt that they were made by hands, but none a human had ever been born with.

"What in God's name did that?" Tracey whispered, breaking the now heavy silence.

"His name was Astaroth. A demon prince I had the misfortune of pissing off. This was his way of saying hello when I got too close to him and interrupted his fun." Karl put his shirt back on. "He had been summoned by a group of cultists in the far North of Minnesota. They called themselves the Disciples of Doomtree. Seven of them in total, or there were, now only three remain. The leader, Lasselbeak, a mad genius had brought then together to take over the world. It was my displeasure to have been in the area when they summoned Astaroth.

"They had no idea the powers they were messing with. I had no idea what I stumbled into. It was a bad scene all the way around. Two of the dumb bastards were consumed immediately. Three more driven insane as he whispered into their minds. I put them down like rabid dogs. But not before they slaughtered an entire town. I was stabbed by the only lady in the group. She'd taken to calling herself Dessa and I fell for her ruse of being an innocent. Astaroth followed my blood into the woods. I was delirious with pain. He seared my wound closed, this one." He pointed to a nasty scar in his right side.

"I tried to crawl away when he gave me those lovely reminders down my back."

"How did you defeat him?" Tracey asked in hushed tones.

Karl laughed mirthlessly. "An angel owed me a favor. Luckily, one of the higher ups. I had to use the boon he granted me for a little job I had done for the Vatican. A one-time deal."

He finished dressing and sat back down at the table. His plate of food had gone cold and was suddenly not nearly as inviting as it had been a short time ago. Jia-Li poured more whiskey into his glass and left the bottle next to it. He greedily drained the glass and poured another. No one spoke as he sat adjusting his tie. He looked across the table and Mikhail nodded at him.

"I feel a bit like an ass now. My apologies, sir."

Karl smiled at him. "Like I said, there is more out there than we can imagine. And not all of it friendly." He drained his glass again and laughed. "I fear I have ruined the evening with my little show. My apologies to the lovely hostess."

Jia-Li smiled at him with teary eyes. "On the contrary, Mr. Beck. You have given me the greatest gift possible. You have proven my faith to be true. In a world of great evil, you have just told me that angels exist. I am filled to the brim with happiness." The tears fell freely down her beautiful face and she seemed to almost glow with joy.

They sat silently and drank for a spell. But, eventually, the conversation resumed on lighter topics. Long into the night they sat talking and laughing. Four new friends sharing with one another. Outside, an owl sat on the roof of the covered porch of the small house. The laughter inside not deterring it from its vigilant watch of the ground beneath. By the time the humans inside had decided it was time to head to their respective beds, it had given up and took flight on soft wings.

10

SOMEWHERE ALONG THE CHISHOLM TRAIL

THE SUN WAS relentless today. All signs of storm two days ago were gone except for scorch marks on the soil. They appeared like etchings from an angry vengeful God. The occasional lost steer or two meandered from tufts of prairie grass. There was no shelter but to hunch among the prickly grass that whipped like razor blades whenever the hot wind gusted. Lizards and snakes patrolled in the welcome heat in search of sustenance from a land they were bred to live in.

One man staggered along the cracked earth, barely upright. He had not stopped moving for a day and a half now. Fear was his biggest motivation against blistered feet rubbed raw in his boots. His thighs chafed from sweating in thick denim. He lost his hat when the winds picked up overnight. Now he had no protection from sun's rays that felt as if they would cook him as he wandered.

"Dear Jesus, please lead your sheep to sanctuary.

Dear Mother Mary, keep that beast from my trail." He repeated the litany to himself, his throat dry and voice cracking.

He needed a drink. Needed food. He hadn't even stopped to relieve himself. He could not close his eyes without seeing that thing launch from the back of the wagon. But Chris was a survivor. A believer. A fighter with a family back in Texas. He could make it to Duncan. He just needed to keep moving.

"God will sustain me. God will protect. I fear no evil for he shelters me in His light. I just need a drink. One drink. Then I can make it."

When night fell, he found he had been running in roughly the right direction. He set his sights on the Big Dipper, found the North Star, and kept moving. As dawn broke to his right, he knew he had not lost his way. Not badly, at least. In the initial panic, he may have gone far to the west or so he guessed. But there wasn't much down the Trail. Duncan was about it and if he stumbled too far past, he would just have to correct his course. But he couldn't think like that. Couldn't afford to. He kept his head up. He had tied his bandana around his forehead. It was something his Pa had taught him. Let it soak up his sweat and cool him down. He laughed bitterly and hoarsely.

"Into your hands, I commend my spirit." The tinge of desperation and insanity in his own voice scared him.

A rabbit leapt from one of the thickets of grass and he felt his heart race in terror. He chuckled to himself and raised a hand to block the sun. In the distance was a cairn of some sort in roughly the direction he stumbled. The adrenaline gave him a burst and his steps evened. He looked up into the azure sky. A lone speck circled high above him. He knew what it was, and he felt another fit of laughter threaten to bubble out. He had seen the devil and there would not be enough of him left for the buzzard above if it caught him.

"Not today, you ugly bastard."

The thicket to his left shook and he watched warily for a moment. Another rabbit, or maybe the same one hopped out and stared at him. He couldn't tell one from another, but he took it as a sign and smiled. It looked at him and bounded off across the hot ground. He watched it skitter across the ground toward another patch of the hardy tall grass. It let out a squeal of horror and he looked up, expecting to see a hawk dive down. He frowned as the only thing he saw was the same buzzard. Then a gray skinned arm snapped out, lightning fast, and grabbed the rabbit and pulled it into the grass. He heard snapping and tearing as he stood still, unable to move.

Then a hissing cackle came out of the shaking brush. *"Ruuuuuuuuuuuuunnnnnnnnnnnnnn . . . "*

Chris stared at the brush, his mouth moving silently, but no sound escaping from his quivering lips. The brush swayed and he felt a warm trickle of piss run down his leg.

Then from the tall grass behind him he heard, *"I said, ruuuuuuuuuuuuunnnnnnnnnnnnnn."*

His body acted as his mind roiled in fear. He took off. Ignoring the blistered feet and cramping calves, he ran as fast as he could, born on pure terror. No thought penetrated the sheer animalistic nature. As he ran the grass around him shook and swayed. He couldn't be sure if it was from the wind or the Devil chasing him. It didn't matter at all. His lungs burned with every wheeze, his body ached. But he knew to stop meant to die. And part of him, the part in control, was not ready for death. As black spots danced around the edge of his vision he kept the cairn in focus.

The Tribes—once many and separate, now few and forced into a small coexistence—sat spread out along the plains. Hides draped over wooden frames dotted the land. Easily dismantled to follow food, they were not sedentary like the Europeans. They had no need for permanent cities. They were like the wind, always moving toward a new destination. But the White man had slowly tied a noose around their necks, made their world smaller and smaller by the day.

Now they roamed the plains of what the Whites called the Indian Region. It was as much prison as open plains. The hardships of The Trail of Tears were still fresh in the elders' minds. Day by day, the old ways were dying off as civilization spreads its hands of death across the land. The trains, belching black smoke, riding on iron rails scared the wildlife. The pitch covered poles strung with thick braided wire for telegraphs traveled from end to end. It looked less like progress, and more the skeletons of the past frozen against once scenic landscapes.

The camp was quiet. Most of the hunters were chasing the herds before the final winter weight was off them. The women sewed hides into clothing with the help of nimble fingered children. In the center, a group of elders gathered around a large dwelling. Each tribe had unique designs painted upon their skin and entered two by two. Inside, the air was smoky from a large fire pit raging in the middle. When all had entered and seated themselves around the fire, they began to pass small leather bags of tobacco. Silence hung as heavy as the smoke in the air as they puffed on their long, intricately carved pipes.

Finally, the silence was broken. The chief of the Muscogee Tribe spoke. "The boy still dreams of the Wendigo. We must prepare for the ceremony before it is too late."

Half the group nodded sagely, while the other half grumbled in discontent. One of the dissenting voices raised. "We should have slain him immediately after River brought him to us. The curse is part of him. None survive a Wendigo unmarked."

"He has shown no signs of the hunger. River watches him. He would not hesitate to take him down like a rabid wolf pup. If we commit to the ceremony, he shall never have to."

"We argue this as foolishly as the boy that stands in the river thinking to stop the flow. Either we do it, or we kill the boy. Enough talk."

"And if it is too late? If he turns?"

"The spirits of the dead shall weep for us if it is too late. We failed to act once, and all remember the price we paid. To let tragedy befall us again due to petty squabbles damns us all."

"Agreed. The moon begins to wane in three days. That is the time for the ritual. We must prepare the inks and purify ourselves first."

HUNGER ON THE CHISHOLM TRAIL

All heads nodded around the great fire. Solemn faces streaked with sweat staring into the flames.

Chris eyed the land warily. He had found open land, with no vegetation. Just the occasional stunted tree stood against the setting sun to his left. He fell to his knees as the last of his strength failed him. He was exhausted. The thirst had grown so that he had no sweat, no tears, his mouth was as dry as the land around him. He needed to keep moving but his legs would not respond. His arms shook as he tried to keep at least on his knees.

Above him, the buzzard still circled, but it had seemed to sense his weakness and come lower to watch closer. He watched it land in the branches of one of the trees. He eyed it as it glared balefully back. He wondered what it would taste like, well aware the big black feathered bastard would have no qualms eating him as well. He found a rock by his hands and threw it at the damned thing.

"Find another meal! I ain't dying here."

It didn't budge at his ineffectual throw. The rock thumped to the ground feet in front of it, limply bouncing near the trunk of the tree. It cocked its head, he swore mockingly, at him and let out an angry screech as if telling him to just curl up and die already.

"Into your hands, I commend my spirit. Please, Christ on your throne, hear my words and deliver me from this evil."

The hot wind picked up again and shook through the leaves of the tree. The buzzard flew back into the sky with one eye always on him. He smiled and felt his lips crack. He wiped his mouth with the back if his hand to see crimson streaks. He struggled to his feet and began to make painful steps forward again. He had never hurt so badly in his life. In his mind, he could see his wife and children back home, waiting for him. He couldn't stop moving. Somewhere ahead of him lay the town of Duncan. A doctor and a priest could heal him. And the sheriff could rally the town against the Devil. He just had to make it.

The wind continued to blow, picking up in intensity. The only good thing was it was blowing at his back and pushing him along. Had it been in his face he would have been powerless against it. He used it to keep moving.

Carried on the wind behind him he swore he heard laughter. He strained his head to listen. And then he heard the howl of something otherworldly. He looked wide eyed as a flash of gray carrying the stench of death blurred past him, felt hot pain as something tore at his cheek and his head snapped, sending a spray of red across the ground. He tumbled from the force of the hit as that same laughter grew louder and louder. Then he heard another terrifying sound. The low rattle and hiss of a rattler. He turned his head to see a coil of brown with diamond like markings on its scales. He just lay there staring at it as the laughter boomed around him. The snake snapped forward and he felt the fangs sink into his hand. He saw the cursed reptile slither away as two red holes in the back of his hand welled up with blood. He could do nothing but stare at it.

"Into your hands, I commend my soul. Into your hands, I commend my soul."

HUNGER ON THE CHISHOLM TRAIL

Over and over he muttered the words as he felt the burning in his hand and across his cheek. Until finally, the wind was knocked from him by the creature as it kicked him in the side. It bent down, the smell worse than anything Chris had smelled since the war when the bodies of the dead and dying were stacked in burial pits by the Negroes and tended to sit bloated in the sun for days before being covered. This thing smelled worse, as if it was born in one of those pits. It was well muscled from the feasting it had over the last few days. But the black eyes showed no compassion, just empty need for more. It bent in close and sniffed at his hand and clucked its tongue in disappointment.

Then it cocked its head and stared into his eyes. *"Innnnntooo your haaaaaaands, innnnntooo yooooooour haaaaaaaands!"* It made the clucking sound again, before letting out another fit of laughter, like iron nails across a tombstone. Chris stared back at it and watched as it just stood and left. He watched it as it ran toward the cairn in the distance.

"Ish headed to Duncan," he slurred before slumping forward to the ground.

The sun was slowly setting and the sky looked as though it had been beaten, with purples and greens etched across it. Across the plains, the stagecoach bounced along the uneven ground, sending a cloud of dust flaring out behind it. The coach driver bounced on the hard wood bench and set the whip cracking in the air above the horses. "C'mon, you mangy bastards! Git! Git!"

A sharp crack rang out into the dusky land. The horses screamed as the weight of coach dragged across the dirt and the rear wheel splintered. Shocked yells came from inside the cab and luggage bounced behind with a tumble of strewn clothes. Isaac fought the reins and managed to bring it to a controlled stop of sorts before the horses were injured.

"God damn this entire trip!" Isaac stared at the ruined wheel and spat a thick, ropy strand of brown.

"My Lord, Isaac! We thoroughly regret the decision of the scenic route. This is twice you've nearly killed us!"

"My apologies, Mr. Harrison, to you and your lovely wife. To you as well, Mr. Barbee, and your missus. It is nothing but a broken wheel. If I could get you gentlemen to help me, we can be on the road in a matter of . . . "

Mr. Harrison leaned his head out of the window. "This shall come out of the expenses. We chose to see the country, not be forced into manual labor every other day."

The four people gingerly stepped out of the awkwardly leaning coach. The ladies let out yells of displeasure as they saw their fineries dotting the filthy ground. They hurried to gather their things before the wind could blow them further abroad.

"Mind yourself, My Petal! Watch for snakes!" Mr. Harrison yelled. He looked around for Isaac but didn't see him by the broken wheel. "Where has that uncouth rapscallion gotten himself off to now?"

"I told you, repeatedly, we should have taken the train. We could have seen the sights from comfort. My ass is a mass of bruises. If not for the brief respite in

Dunkirk, I fear I would have forgotten even a modicum of civilized life in this accursed wagon." Mr. Barbee stared at the ladies as they gathered up the clothes. He smiled slightly as the wind gusted and blew their skirts up as they frantically chased bloomers and petticoats. But the smile quickly faded as he saw the woman on her horse pull up. The filthy mouthed outlaw woman dared sit astride her horse and laugh at them.

Mr. Harrison ignore the jabs of his business partner, something he had honed to an art over the years. "Isaac, damn you man, where have you gotten yourself off to?"

"Over here, sirs! I've found something terrible!"

"What now?" Mr. Barbee cursed under his breath, "Damn fool. We need to be making up time, not exploring this desolate hell."

The men carefully navigated a dried stream bed and found Isaac standing over a corpse. Mr. Harrison let out a low whistle and Mr. Barbee took off his top hat and held it over his chest.

"I seen a vulture sitting in the tree staring mighty hard at the ground. I think he may yet live."

Chris lay still on the ground, his chest barely rising in labored breaths. His hand was swollen to near twice the size of normal. Dark blood crusted upon his cheek.

Isaac bent down and gently shook his chest. "Mister? You alive still, mister?" Chris let out a low moan that caused all three men to jump a little.

The sound of hooves signaled Mary Jo riding up. "What in tarnation? He still livin?"

Isaac opened his mouth to answer but Mr.

Harrison cut him off before he could. "No. The poor bastard has been bitten and clawed. I fear he must have expired sometime earlier. Isaac saw a vulture about to feast upon his poor bones. No time to dilly-dally, though. Life is short as this poor soul found out. We must fix the wheel and get to moving while we have the little light that remains!"

Mr. Barbee looked at him shrewdly and nodded. "Yes. I fear the time has passed for him, but not for us. Back to work, gentlemen."

Isaac stared hard at them and gave a look to Mary Jo that was plaintive at best. She turned to face the men that were sidling away. "As good Christians, surely you will at least bury the poor bastard, right?"

They looked at each other with a sour expression. Mr. Barbee sighed, "Madame, clearly we have no shovel. Nor other means to inter a corpse. What we have is a coach with a broken wheel and fading sunlight. While I feel quite sorry for the poor bastard, I fail to see how it is my or my partner's responsibility. These are perilous times we live in and we cannot be expected to travel the country burying every corpse we stumble upon. Feel free to do it yourself, if you are so inclined. We have other business to attend to."

Mr. Harrison looked slightly uncomfortable with the entire situation. But he simply tipped his hat to Mary Jo and gave Isaac the stink eye. As Isaac moved to follow, the hand of the not so deceased snapped up and gripped his pants. Everyone froze.

"Have to warn them," Chris slurred.

"Warn who?" Mary Jo asked.

"Duncan. It's headed to Duncan. Killed

everyone . . . " his arm slumped back down to the ground.

Mary Jo rounded on the two men. "You sacks of shit! You knew! You would have let him die and not thought a damned thing about it!"

Mr. Barbee held up his hands. "I assure you we did not! Look at him. He seemed obviously dead. I don't quite care for your tone. Not one bit. Your accusation is an affront to mine and my partner's honor!"

He leapt into the air as a bullet hit the ground less than a foot in from of him. He stared wide eyed at Mary Jo who sat with her revolver trained on him. "An affront to your honor? What honor, you lily livered chicken shit? I'm a fair shot and I bet I can shoot you in the honor, or at least in the pecker."

Mr. Harrison raised his hand in a placating gesture. "Now ma'am, I'm sure there is no reason for violence. It was a mistake. An honest one. Clearly that man will be among the angels soon. Forgive us for being city folk unaccustomed to the life on the prairie."

"You both speak awfully pretty. I'm sure you're right. You would do anything to take care of this poor soul had ya known he was still alive. Ain't that right?"

They both nodded vigorously.

"Good ta hear it. Isaac, I'm gonna need one of your horses. I'll take this poor sonovabitch back to Duncan to the doctor."

Mr. Barbee stomped his foot on the hard ground. "Now wait just a good god damned minute! We can't go a horse short! You'll trap us out here!"

"It'll take me a day to get to Duncan and drop him off. A day back. Then you can take yer yellow ass to wherever chickenshits go to roost." She raised the gun again. "Or is that an issue you feel the need to argue?"

"You treacherous who . . . "

"I suggest you choose that next word very carefully, boy. My finger's gettin' a mite itchy."

"Take the damned horse. Fine. It's extortion under the threat of violence, is what it is."

"Fancy word for you'll get your pecker shot off if'n you don't do the right thing."

Mr. Barbee mumbled to himself but didn't say anything else. His hands slowly moved down to protect his crotch, though. Isaac ran ahead to free one of the horses. And Mr. Harrison managed to look suitably ashamed of himself.

"Now, if you gentleman can help Isaac when he returns to get this poor bastard onto the horse. I'll be off as quickly as I can. Gotta get back quick as lightning so you don't get scared of the great outdoors."

Isaac returned rather swiftly with one of the mares. The three of them managed to get Chris up and over the back of the horse. Isaac used ropes to secure his unconscious body in place.

Mary Jo grinned and shot the ground by Mr. Barbee who leapt to the side with both hands clutching his family jewels. "Y'all take care and try not to let the coyotes eat ya. I'll be back in two days or so. And Mr. Barbee?" He glared at her and she laughed to see the front of his pants stained a darker color than the rest. "You may want to tell your wife I saw one of her bustles blowin' down the Ridgeline."

With that, she took the lead of the other horse,

clucked her tongue and rode off. A cloud of dust and her laughter rang out as she sped away.

"Not a word to the ladies, Mr. Harrison."

Mr. Harrison looked at him with a grin. "Of course not, Mr. Barbee."

11

DUNCAN

"IT WAS THE most amazing thing I ever witnessed," Amber was telling Marie. Marie nodded, having heard the story at least forty times at this point and kept wiping off the tables. "Tate the Great selected me! Said I was the prettiest girl he ever did see. Let me and my brother wrap the chains around his arms. My brother din't believe the chains was real. But sure as I am sitting here they was!"

The problem with a brothel in the middle of nowhere was that business was slower than spit in winter. The girls had nothing to do but drink and entertain the locals who mostly were married men and drunkards. But everyone was excited at the prospect of the first drive rolling in any minute. The bar would be lively, and the girls would be using their mouths for things other than talking. Marie couldn't wait for the last bit. A stop over two summers ago to make some quick cash serving drivers for Kenzie on her way to Texas had turned into a full-time job.

114

Robert at the post office was to blame for that mostly. Even if he was too stupid to realize it.

"So we locked the four heavy locks . . . " Amber continued.

"To put him in a box and toss him into the god damned river. Lord Above, Amber, how many times will you tell us this same cockamamie story? Sixty seconds later, he was on the bank," Tara finished with a huff.

"I lost the chain, but I'll be damned if I was gonna lose the locks as well." Brad, Kenzie and Marie said in unison. They all began laughing as Amber rolled her eyes.

Bella sat watching. That is what she did mostly. Her English was not very good, her thick Italian accent and sultry dark looks more than making up for her silence. She smiled as everyone laughed. Watching both Frank and Oliver, the men that came to town late last evening watching her. She found both repugnant, but knew their money spent just as well as anyone else's. She batted her eyes at them and saw Frank, the overweight one, flush scarlet. She'd hoped for him, the lesser of two evils. Oliver had cold, flat eyes that she didn't care for. She'd come to recognize those as the type to belong to someone that enjoyed inflicting pain. No, he was more Tara's type.

Josiah and Teddy sat huddled together at one of the faro tables, Josiah whispering and Teddy nodding while knocking back red eye as fast as he poured them. At this rate, he would stumble out back to puke his guts out before the fat red sun finished setting.

"So Bradley, how did that outlaw treat you before she took off?" Kenzie asked loudly, an evil grin on her face as she did. "Seems to me there was an awful lot of yelling going on up there."

Bradley maintained his composure though he managed to blush and look green in the gills at the same time. "A gentleman doesn't share what happens between he and a lady in the bedroom."

"Well she sure as shit weren't no lady and you damned well ain't no gentleman! Spill it, old man!" Tara shouted. Even Amber stopped pouting and leaned forward to hear the tale.

Marie set her rag on the table and watched with a grin like the cat that stole the canary. "Did she paint yer picture?"

Bradley tried to look above such talk and nearly managed. "Twasn't my picture she painted." Everyone cackled and hooted at him. "And I agree, she most certainly wasn't a lady. I'm still trying to get all the paint off."

"She must have needed a fine point brush if she painted down there," Kenzie said to more laughter.

"It isn't about the brush, it's the brush strokes," he quipped back.

Kenzie opened her mouth for a rebuttal when the door to the bar crashed open. Every face turned and stared slack-jawed as Mary Jo yelled, "Someone fetch the sawbones! I got an injured man out here!"

Kenzie pointed to Bella and she nodded and fled through the open door and down the street. "Bradley, you and Marie see about getting the man upstairs."

They both stood and hurried outside. Mary Jo followed and used her long blade to cut the ropes. As she did, Chris slid from the horse's back and Bradley grunted as he barely stopped him from hitting the ground. Marie grabbed his legs and they made their way back inside. Chris's head lolled to the side and he let out a fevered moan.

Kenzie watched in concern as they struggled to get him up the stairs and into one of the vacant rooms. "What happened to him?"

Mary Jo shrugged. "Found him half dead yesterday. Snake bite on his hand, I reckon. Something clawed his face up good."

"Coyote or wolf?"

"Ain't never seen one like that. Looks more like a bear but ain't none of them in these here parts."

Kenzie nodded. "He looks familiar. Tara or Amber, either of you know him?" They both shook their heads. "How about you, Josiah?"

Josiah turned with a start and bleary eyes. "Whassat?"

"Damn drunk. I asked if you recognized the poor bastard we just hauled in. Looks near death. Maybe you can sober up enough to administer last rites if necessary? Not to disturb your drinking at all."

"Listen here, you heathen!" he shouted. Then he saw all the angry stares and quickly shut his mouth. Teddy watched and poured himself an extra large glass of red eye.

He was saved further embarrassment as the door opened and Cody came rushing in. Not far behind him were Mikhail and Karl. Cody took the stairs two at a time. Karl followed him while Mikhail stopped and nodded to Mary Jo.

"Ma'am."

"I was just telling them. We stumbled on his body a day's hard ride to the South. Thought he was dead.

117

Snake bit hand and clawed up face. I took one of the coach's horses and made due haste here."

"Anyone know the man?"

Kenzie shook her head. "Not so far as we could tell. The good preacher was just about to head upstairs and see if he can do anything to help. Isn't that right, Josiah?"

Josiah finished his drink and nodded. "Yes sir, sheriff. I'm headed that way now." He stumbled a bit as he took a few shaky steps. Mikhail followed him up the stairs.

Mary Jo looked at Bradley and winked. He made a point of turning away as his face flared up red.

Cody examined Chris and shook his head. "I fear the arm is lost to the elbow. The swelling and necrosis have gone too far. He was of sound enough mind at some point to tie his belt off at his forearm."

Karl nodded. "Those claw marks on his face concern me. They fester but seem far too fresh."

Cody reached into his bag and pulled out a tongue depressor and ran it along one of the four ragged wounds. A thick discharge oozed out of the wound. He frowned at it and sniffed. "It carries the scent of death."

Karl frowned and retrieved a metal vial from his pocket and took a sample. "This is unusual indeed."

Josiah entered the room with Mikhail right behind him. Josiah's eyes grew big. "That's Chris. He is one of the cattlemen from Texas."

Mikhail frowned. "A cattleman alone in the

middle of nowhere? That don't add up. Has he spoke?" Cody and Karl shook their heads.

"He said someone was headed to Duncan. That he killed everyone. He ain't spoke since." Mary Jo stood in the doorway. "He didn't say who was killed nor who did the killin'. Hell's bells, it probably weren't nothin' but the fever talkin'. I heard ya say he is a cattleman. There weren't hide nor hair of steer around that I saw. Just him layin' on the ground near dead. Poor bastard. Them city slickers would have left him fer dead. Ain't right."

"You seen any tracks? Any sign of a struggle? Smell anything unusual? Like rotten eggs, perhaps. Or see any sign of frost on the plants?" Karl asked quietly.

"I reckon I'da told ya if'n any weird shit like that had happened. It's a snake bite. Makes a person see some strange things. Once my pal got bit and spent three days in a fever talking to his dead pa."

Cody nodded. "Delirium can occur with a high enough fever. Now I need one of you to stay with me and assist me in the procedure. The quicker his arm is removed, the more likely his chances of survival."

Josiah stepped forward on wobbly legs and knelt next to the bed. "Our Father, I ask that you give comfort to this lamb. I beseech the Holy Spirit to protect this man. His sacred covenant with you is unbreakable, even in the face of death."

Chris's eyes snapped open and he turned his head weakly towards Josiah. "It was the devil, father. The devil came for me . . . " And with that he spoke his last. A wheezing rattle escaped his chest and he moved no more.

Cody put two fingers onto his throat and shook his head sadly. "He is gone."

Karl stared at the corpse with a frown. Mikhail and Mary Jo made the sign of the cross as Josiah mumbled a prayer of guidance for his soul to reach heaven.

"Well shit. I guess I didn't make it in time at all. I need a whiskey and a hard fucking from a tall bartender before I hit the saddle again." With that, Mary Jo left the room.

Mikhail looked at Karl. "The Devil?"

Karl shook his head. "None of the signs. No. I fear this man just got bit as the good doctor said. Though it is most peculiar. Most peculiar indeed."

Cody shrugged. "You gentleman mind helping me get him downstairs? I'd like to examine his body as soon as possible before rigor mortis sets in."

Josiah stood and looked at Cody. "This man is a good Christian. Don't go desecrating his corpse to further your godless science. He will get a proper funeral. Teddy and I will take care of him."

Cody looked disappointed but shrugged. It wasn't worth the fight. "Well, would you two gentlemen care for a few glasses of whiskey? I've developed a thirst."

Karl looked at Mikhail. "Whiskey sounds good to me."

Mikhail looked at him and cocked his head. "You okay?"

Karl stared off into space for a long silent moment. "Been a strange week. Ever since that stranger came through town I've felt like something is brewing."

"The guy looking for Dust?"

"James Dee."

"Think he did that?" Mikhail pointed into the room."

"No. He is a different kind of devil. He would not have left Chris alive. It's most likely nothing. Just something feels off."

"Maybe you're just nervous about your day with Tracey tomorrow night."

Karl smiled. "Maybe that's it. It has been a while."

"Let's get that drink."

One drink led to quite a few drinks. The solemn day began to unwind as the moon rose over Duncan. Mikhail and Karl sat at the bar with a bottle of Kenzie's best reserves.

"No summoning demons in my establishment, Mr. Beck." She gave him a slight smile.

"He was trying to protect you. Karl is a hero. And my wife is quite happy to have made his acquaintance. Says he is a proper gentleman."

Karl snorted. "Your lovely wife is an angel. Yet somehow misguided on this point."

Amber could not take her eyes off of the strange Mr. Beck. He was intelligent, yet seemed so down to earth with a hint of mystery that got her excited in ways the cattlemen did not. She couldn't recall the last time she wanted a man, not his coin or drink. But to be taken by one freely. Tara looked across the room and saw the hunger in her eyes. She raised an eyebrow at her and nodded, encouraging her. Amber met her gaze and smiled. She stood and smoothed her skirt, awash with nervousness. "I trust the sheriff's wife. She is a very good judge of character."

Karl looked at her in surprise. "Jia-Li is wise indeed. Even if her taste in men seems suspect." Mikhail and Kenzie roared with laughter.

Amber joined them at the bar and Brad poured her a glass of wine. She swirled it gently in the cup and took a sip to wet her lips. Then she leaned forward and placed her wine sweet lips upon Karl's. A roar filled the room as he sat stunned.

No one noticed the small cry of alarm from behind them as Tracey stood in shock. She turned and ran from the doorway with tears welling in the corner of her eyes. She fled too soon to see Karl gently push Amber away. In her haste to escape, she never heard his admonishments. All she saw was the man she had thought perhaps, just maybe, could be the one to unlock the chains she had wrapped so tightly around her heart all those years ago.

She ran back to her shop and slammed the lock closed. She turned away from the street and stood with her back against the closed sign. Two days ago, she made the choice to stop taking Laudanum. To let her head clear and her heart heal. She felt like a damn fool. Crying over a stranger that would leave town in a few days and never think of her again.

"Hope is poison," she muttered through ragged breathing.

She walked to the shelf and grabbed a fresh bottle of her only need. She ran her trembling lips across the glass straw, felt the numbness soak into her sorrow. It slowly faded. A dull throb now. She dipped it back into the bottle and let it run down the back of her throat. She didn't need anyone or anything. She had proven it to herself many times over. Loneliness was freedom. She embraced it.

"It's all shit. All of it. Happy endings are for stories. For fools and poets." She heard the slur in her voice. Felt her legs grow weary and she just let herself slide down the door to sit on the floor. Her mind was fuzzy.

Then she heard a noise upstairs The wind outside had picked up and she couldn't remember if she shut the window this morning. She found it hard to remember this morning. All she could see was Amber kissing Karl as the room went wild.

"Could have kissed me that way. A cheap harlot is his style, is she? I hope he gets the drip from her. Serves them both right."

She pushed herself off the floor and made her way unsteadily to the stairs, the bottle clutched in her hand. Her eyes were unfocused and she missed the bottom step twice before finally finding it.

"Damned things keep moving." She laughed at her own joke and gripped the wall firmly as she made her way up. The curtain fluttered in the wind and her modest book collection lay scattered on the floor. She kicked the books under the bed before collapsing on top of it herself.

"Here is to not needing anyone. Especially not you, Karl Beck, with your scars and pretty eyes." She let two fat drops of Laudanum land on her tongue and smiled blearily at the ceiling. The room smelled terrible and she guessed it was a skunk that had crept in. The how and why a skunk would scale the side of the building didn't matter to her much in this state.

It was an answer to a problem she couldn't focus on. One that made as much sense as anything. Like Karl leading her on the last week.

A scrabbling sound from under the bed caught her attention. She lit the lantern on the counter, it only took three tries, a feat she felt oddly proud of and called, "Back out the window, varmint. I don't have the will nor capacity to deal with you."

The scrabbling grew louder and she leaned over the edge to see what had gotten into her room. Her head seemed far too heavy and she found herself in a pile on the floor. She laughed at the ridiculousness of the situation. A long belly laugh that tinged on the edge of insane. Then she turned her head to look beneath the bed itself.

Two black eyes stared out of a gray face with a rictus grin. She blinked in confusion, thinking it would simply vanish.

"Who are you?" she asked what she was sure was a figment of her imagination.

The black eyes blinked, they seemed darker than the shadows cast as the breeze made the lantern flame dance on the windowsill above. "You're not really there are you, Mr. Monster? You're just a shadow and I'm too sleepy to play with you."

She got to her knees with an effort. A small snort escaped her as she realized she may have gone overboard with her numbing of her mind. Slowly she stood up and fell spellbound staring at the flame in the lantern. Something grabbed her foot and she tried to kick it away. It tightened its grip like a steel band and she found herself pulled back down onto her back with a tremendous thump. The breath left her with a loud whoosh. She turned and stared down her body at the gray hand on her ankle and tried to feebly fight back.

"Cooooooooome untooooooooo meeeeeeeee."

A startled yelp came out of her mouth as she felt herself slide under the bed. She found herself face to face with monster under the bed and opened her mouth to scream as it drove its fist into her side. She found herself unable to finish the scream as blood filled her lung. It's dark smile was the last thing she saw as a mouth filled with jagged teeth came across the floor and sank into her soft flesh.

Hasse Ola let out a scream of pain and crumbled into a heap on the floor of the small building. River leapt to his feet and ran to him as his body began convulsing. His muscles rippled under his skin and his eyes rolled back in his head as he thrashed about. River looked frantically about the room and grabbed the ledger in which he recorded the taxes and tore the cover off.

He went to shove the leather into Hasse's mouth but froze as he heard the young man speak for the first time in their three years together. His back arched and with a painful scream, "Wiiiiiiiiiiindeeeeeegoooooo!"

He stared in fright at his companion. Then scooped him off of the ground with a grunt and ran outside. The town of Duncan sat quietly in front of him as he placed Hasse Ola over the horse's back and leapt astride himself. Without a second look, he rode off to where the tribes had gathered, praying to the spirits it wasn't already too late.

12

DUNCAN

KARL WOKE WITH a pounding headache and a mouth that felt packed with cotton. He looked around, unable to get his bearings. The sour smell of liquor wafted into his nose and he felt his stomach lurch. He had passed out in Kenzie's. Or, basically, had before stumbling upstairs and barely getting his boots off. He covered his eyes with his arm to block the sun that felt like knives going from his eyes into his brain. He remembered a good portion of the evening. Or enough bits and pieces to wonder at the foolhardy attempt to drink all of the whiskey in the bar. And dancing, or at least spinning round and round between with the ladies. His face flushed as the memory of Amber kissing him long and hard came back. Her rushing off and eventually coming back down. He was sure they had talked it over.

Mikhail was in just as bad a shape. He had an image of Jia-Li staring disappointedly at them as they sat by the piano singing off key and far too loudly. She seemed less than courteous as she escorted him from

126

the building. He pitied him if he woke in the same state. Karl was sure Jia-Li would be making a racket in the quaint little home this morning.

"Mr. Beck, are you among the living?" Kenzie called from downstairs. "If you are so inclined, you are welcome to join us for the morning meal."

"I am not dead yet, even though I may slightly wish I were, madam. I shall be down as soon as I regain use of my limbs. Thank you."

"You seemed to have lost the control of your limbs last night. You are the single worst dancer I ever did see. Rivaled only by your singing voice," Tara called up.

He smiled, which somehow sent a fresh wave of pain through his system. He wanted to curl up in a ball for the rest of the day. And then he sat with a start as he remembered his date with Tracey this evening. His nausea was replaced with a hammering heart. He still ached, but adrenaline surged and he was able to get his boots on and head downstairs.

"He lives!" Bradley shouted sending stars at the edge of his vision.

"Looks as if he wishes he didn't," Amber added.

The smell of sizzling bacon set his mouth to watering as his stomach did uncertain somersaults. They laid at a veritable feast compared to the simple oats he had been eating at the sheriff's office every morning. He sat down gingerly as Kenzie scooped eggs and bacon and a medley of veggies onto a plate for him.

"I thank you kindly, ma'am, not just for the meal but the evenings libations and fun as well."

She smiled. "We may have gotten off on the wrong

foot earlier. But Mikhail and Jia-Li like you, and it was truly an unfortunate misunderstanding. None of us knew demon hunting was a real profession. Seems only fair."

"So, you write, I recall you telling me about that last night."

She blushed. Bradley spoke up, "Best damn storyteller I've ever heard."

Kenzie smiled and patted Bradley's cheek. She opened her mouth to speak when the door to the bar slammed open. Everyone turned and saw Mikhail standing there looking like death worked over.

"Has anyone spoken to Tracey today?" he asked with concern in his voice.

A chorus of no's answered him. And he looked at Karl, "You haven't spoken to her today?"

Karl shook his head. "I just woke up. What's going on?"

Mikhail walked over and took a piece of bacon off of his plate. "Jia wanted me to get her some canned peaches this morning."

Karl raised an eyebrow.

"She woke me up before the sun had risen by banging a pot in the kitchen."

"She seemed less than enthusiastic about our antics last night."

"She never mentioned it this morning. But she suddenly had chores for me that needed done immediately. She is very beautiful, loving and whip smart. But she does not tolerate fools. Apparently, I made a fool of myself last night."

"Hard labor works the stupid out," Marie said with a smile. Then she looked at Bradley, "Most of the time, at least."

Karl sat staring at his food and played with his eggs with his fork as everyone laughed. The mood was light, but he had a sinking feeling in his guts. "What about Tracey?"

"She never answered when I went to get the peaches. I banged on the door pretty loudly. Rob said he saw her coming toward the bar last night as he was headed on his evening stroll."

All eyes turned toward Marie who blushed. Everyone knew she found an excuse to sneak out with him on his evening strolls. "We did see her headed toward the bar last night. But I was . . . otherwise preoccupied."

Tara snorted. "Too polite to talk with your mouth full, Marie?" Amber nearly fell from her seat laughing. And Marie's mouth moved up and down soundlessly for a moment. "Looks about right," she added with a second snort.

"What time was this?" Karl asked with an intensity that silenced the banter.

"Not sure. An hour after we all came down. After, you know . . . " Marie said.

Karl's stomach dropped. Mikhail saw his expression and looked at Amber. He made the same face. Karl stood up and put on his jacket. And the two of them left the bar without a word.

"Oh no," Amber muttered. "You don't think she saw me . . . "

Kenzie didn't say a word. No one did. Everyone knew of Tracey's troubled past. Not the specifics. It was the big gossip around town when she was seen walking with Karl.

Bella patted her on the shoulder. "Surely it is a coincidence. That is all."

Karl practically ran to the shop. Mikhail was right behind him. Karl began banging on the door while Mikhail went around back and did the same. There was no sign of movement inside at all.

"I'm going to break out the window!" Karl yelled.

"Wait a minute! I noticed the window upstairs is open earlier. She could be sleeping heavily. Or out for a walk. No need destroying a perfectly good window if we don't have to." He walked back around and pointed at the open window.

Karl and he pushed a couple barrels next to the building. Then they stacked crates on top of them. Then he nodded and climbed onto the barrels. "Hold these crates steady for me."

"You sure you want to do this, old timer?"

"Hellfire and damnation, I've been exploring crypts since before you were off your Mama's teat. Just hold them steady."

He scampered up and onto the covered porch and made his way to the open window. The stench of death attacked his nose immediately. "Tracey! Can you hear me?"

He covered his mouth with a bandana and felt the previous evening rolling about in his stomach. He climbed into the window and froze as he saw the large patch of crimson pooled. He leaned down and dipped his finger into it. Cold and thick, not fresh. By the shade and consistency, he placed it at last night. He carefully got down onto his knees and looked under the bed. His heart stopped as he saw the shredded remains of Tracey staring back at him. Her body was in tatters, but her face had been left alone. He got to his feet and staggered down the stairs. He felt tears leaking down his cheeks, but years of horrible scenes had numbed his brain. Something had done this to her. He could focus on sadness later. Now he had a goal. A creature that needed put down.

He unlocked the front door and opened it. Mikhail saw his expression and his face fell into misery. He opened his mouth to speak but Karl shook his head and walked to the side of the porch. The entire contents of last night, mostly bile and stomach acid, rained down onto the ground. He retched until he was empty and then for a few more moments for good measure.

"She's dead." It was all he could manage. Her sad eyes, now empty of light, filled his mind.

"Laudanum?"

Karl shook his head. "No. She looked half eaten."

"Eaten? Ain't no predator except a bobcat that could get up there."

"Wrong kind of predator."

Mikhail walked inside as Karl leaned on the railing. Karl took in several gulps of air and wiped his cheeks and mouth with his handkerchief. He looked down the street and saw Kenzie and Bradley standing in the dirt staring at him. Kenzie turned to Bradley and seemed to be sobbing as he wrapped his arms around her and gently patted her back. Karl felt ice in his guts and went back inside.

Mikhail had flipped the mattress of the bed and the remains of Tracey showed through the slats of wood. He looked a little green around the edges as his mind tried to process what he was seeing. Her breasts had been clawed to shreds. Her stomach was torn open and there were clear bite marks where the flesh had been ripped off with teeth. Her left leg was gnawed so that splinted ivory bone was exposed. Her ribs cracked off and the marrow seemed to have been sucked out of the discarded bone.

"She was meant to be found. That's why it left her face untouched." Karl heard the ice in his own voice. He half expected to see frost leave his mouth and dance upon the stale air.

"What could have done this?"

Karl stared. "No ghoul or zombic, the head would have been crushed and the brains devoured. Whatever this was enjoyed itself. It's consumed by hunger and driven to violence."

"A man?"

"No. Look, her genitals aren't touched at all. She wasn't raped. Wasn't desecrated. This was pure vehement rage and need."

"A monster? Did you bring a monster to my quiet town?" Mikhail spoke softly, disbelief in the face of what he was seeing at war with an understanding that his world was suddenly darker. Anger seemed to bubble over his words.

"I don't bring monsters, Mikhail. I kill them."

"That stranger, Dee, he looked capable of this."

"Dee kills monsters as well. And has been gone near a week. No man did this."

"What do we do?"

"We find it. We kill it. We burn whatever remains."

"I need to check on Jia-Li. And the rest of the town, as well."

Karl nodded. "Gather up the men. We need to search every inch of town. Get as many people to the bar as possible. It's central. They can keep an eye on one another."

Mikhail didn't move. He just stared at what used to be his friend. Karl could guess at the war in his mind. His mind went back to Vermont. He saw his family slaughtered. Heard the otherworldly laughter as the thing with tentacles and claws disemboweled his brother as he lay under the bed. Old scars flared with burning along his thigh.

"Now, Sheriff. Move."

Mikhail snapped out of thought and turned toward the stairs. "Meet you at the jail in an hour."

"I will see if I can figure out what did this. We need to check on the Natives as well. They are far enough outside of town that they could be in danger."

Mikhail nodded and hurried down the stairs. He'd head straight home, Karl figured. Make sure Jia-Li was okay before heading around town. He didn't blame him. His first stop would have been . . . here. To make sure Tracey was okay. Instead he had been getting soused at the bar. Instead he had been kissed by Amber. Did she see that? Is that why she never came in?

He shook his head. Banished all thought. He pulled at the slats and the nails holding them popped from the frame. He felt splinters enter his hands but he didn't care, didn't stop until she was free of the wooden bars. Then he took the comforter off the floor where Mikhail had flipped the mattress and gently set it over her.

"I truly wish we had gotten our date, ma'am. Like

you wouldn't believe. I had taken a shine to you, one I haven't felt in many a year. I will get this son of a bitch. And I will make it pay. I promise you."

He reached down and closed her eyes. Her skin was cold but felt soft beneath his callused hands. Then he turned and walked down the stairs without a glance back. Hell seemed to tremble beneath his boots as he walked down the stairs and into the sunlight.

The front door slammed open and Jia-Li stood with her hands on her hips and a serious expression on her face. "How far did you have to go for those peaches? Georgia?"

Then she saw the look on her puppy's face. Her stern look melted away and she rushed to him. He wrapped his arms around her and squeezed for all he was worth. The breath in her chest fled at the force of it. She felt him tremble as he held her and she melted into him. All other emotion fled as her concern grew.

Finally, he let go. Not completely, but enough that she felt her chest fill with air. She looked up and saw tears. "Pup, what happened?"

"It's Tracey."

"What about her? Is she back on that poison?"

"No, my love. She is dead."

"I knew that garbage would kill her one day. I had such hope that Karl would be the one to pull her away from it."

"It wasn't the Laudanum. She was murdered. Eaten."

"Wolfs?"

"No. Not wolves. Something else. Karl thinks it is a monster come to Duncan."

She pulled away and grabbed the rifle from over the mantle and sighted down the barrel. "Then we must find it. Someone else could be in jeopardy."

He pushed the barrel of the rifle toward the ground and took her gently by the wrist. "We will. I need you to go to Kenzie's. Safety in numbers. I'll gather some of the men. Bradley, Robert, Karl, maybe River and Hasse Ola too. We'll find it."

She looked at him stubbornly. "I am a better shot than all of you. You need me."

"I need you to protect the others."

She squinted her eyes and gave him a long look. Then she nodded. "It makes sense. Take your extra revolver. I cleaned it two days ago and oiled it. You take such bad care of it."

He smiled. "I have you to take care of it."

She returned his smile and then rushed to him and kissed him long and deep. "You take care of you. We go to California soon. Don't make me save your life. I love you, Pup."

He lifted her chin and stared into those perfect brown eyes. "You already did, my love. Now get to the bar. Tell Kenzie what is happening. Have Bradley meet Karl at the jail. I love you too."

She nodded and grabbed a box of ammunition from the shelf and left as he went to the bedroom and got his spare revolver. He smiled at it as it gleamed. She really had recently cleaned it and wrapped it in an oilskin.

Karl sat pouring over the books he had stored in his worn saddlebags. He searched for cannibalistic creatures that exuded the smell of death. He made notes on the back of a wanted poster as he went. Then he cross referenced in a few grimoires and mythology journals he had gathered. Nothing made sense. There was malevolence to the act as well as a hunger. Her turned face staring out from under the bed burnt into his mind as he tried to focus.

Bradley walked into the jail and cringed at the expression Karl shot at him. "We are all just gutted by this, Mr. Beck. Truly. "

"We will be gutted if I don't figure out what it is." He looked angrily at the books scattered around him. "I have nothing. Not a damned thing that helps."

Bradley took off his hat and clutched it nervously. "You think it was the same thing that got the cattleman?"

Karl laughed bitterly. "Most likely."

"So the Devil himself has come to Duncan." Bradley made the sign of the cross.

"The Devil himself rarely has a need to go anywhere. There is enough evil on the planet without him. This is not the Devil. This is a vermin that needs to be eradicated."

Bradley nodded, but his eyes showed doubt. He walked over and sat in an empty chair and watched as Karl flipped through pages and scribbled notes. The fear he felt was dwarfed in the magnitude of resolve he felt pouring off of Karl Beck. He suddenly felt as if not even the Devil could stand up to this man.

Mikhail walked with purpose down the main street. There was no need to saddle a horse for the trip. In fact it would make it take longer, he decided, as he nearly jogged down the street with his hand clutching the handle of his revolver.

He saw Cody sitting in his office. He stopped his frantic pace and stared at him in confusion. He sat in a chair and was just staring at his hand in wonder with a dazed expression. He walked up to the door and opened it slowly.

"I take it word has not gotten to you yet?"

He blinked at Mikhail for a second. "What happened?"

"Tracey is dead. Murdered in the night. Karl is at the jail and I'm gathering a group to search town for the killer."

"Tracey is what?"

"Dead, Cody. We found her this morning. Half eaten and stuffed under her bed."

Cody began laughing hysterically. "I very nearly believed you!"

Mikhail stared at him in shock before he slapped him in the mouth. "It is not a laughing matter. Pull yourself together, man!"

Cody held his cheek. "Wha . . . why? Tracey is really dead? Eaten? By what? Bobcat?" His words sounded thick and syrupy. Almost dreamlike.

"What's gotten into you, sawbones?"

"Nothing. I'm fine. Just tired." His mind raced in odd directions. The mushrooms he had eaten dragged him along. Opened him to new paths of thought. But made it hard to concentrate on the here and now. "What do you need me to do?"

"Head to the jail. We need to search every inch of Duncan."

"Where is Tracey's body now? I'd like to examine her if possible. For science."

"There will be time for that after we know the city is safe."

"Yes, yes. You're right. I'll head to the jail immediately."

Mikhail still eyed him with concern but patted him on the shoulder. "I am sorry for the slap. It was too far."

Cody just shook his head. "Think nothing of it, Sheriff. Better than a cup of coffee for shaking the cobwebs loose. You ever stare at a web? The intricate design is unique to each spider. Did you know that?"

"I didn't. Perhaps after this is all over you can join Jia-Li and I for dinner. She enjoys talking with you."

"That would be wonderful. Thank you."

Mikhail nodded and walked out as Cody gathered his things. He had always found Cody to be strange, but Jia-Li said it was a sign of genius. He just thought he was strange. But he knew his business of healing, even if his methods seemed weird.

He kept walking down the street. Josiah and Teddy were outside the church. Josiah gave him a curt nod and Teddy spat in the dirt.

"We were just discussing tragedy, sheriff. May God shelter her soul in his loving embrace. We, of course, will do whatever we can to help. Your lovely wife mentioned meeting at the jail and we were just conversing about heading down there." Josiah almost sounded convincing. Teddy looked like he might bolt at any second.

"I appreciate that. I'm going to get Robert, then check on River and Hasse Ola. If you have any weapons, bring them."

"Them savages most likely did it." Teddy looked to Josiah, who nodded sagely. "Or some of them from the council. They ain't big on us palefaces. We should ride out there and get our payback for them killing her."

"Already drinking, Teddy? It wasn't a human that did what was done to her. Just keep your opinion to yourself and get to the jail."

"You'll see. They ain't like us."

"That will do, Teddy. The sheriff is busy."

"I'm just sayin' is all. It was you that done brought me to the light. Opened my eyes to the evils of the red skinned devils. I bet it was them that did in Chris, too. Damned savages."

"You need to put a leash on your dog there, Josiah. We got enough to deal with as it is." Mikhail glared at the two of them. No one cared for either of them. But Josiah swa the preacher, and that carried a certain weight. Teddy was just scum that clung to him for free drinks and the occasional pew to sleep on.

"Apologies, sheriff. Let us gather our things and we will be there shortly. This evil will be purged as the Lord commands."

Mikhail didn't respond. He passed Kenzie's and saw Jia-Li taking control inside. Even Kenzie herself was doing as she motioned. He smiled for the briefest moment. She was literally the most competent leader he had ever known. She carried herself with severity when there was a job to be done. But she laughed and joked like one of the guys when they were alone. He was constantly amazed at the pure joy of her, the light she brought into his life. He wasn't good with words or emotions, but he did everything he could to show her his deep affection. Even if he wasn't always sure he deserved her. She was his everything. His rock in the midst of turmoil.

He nearly walked past the post office in his reverie, but caught himself at the last moment. The door to the post office was open. Robert sat stoically at his desk like he always did but smiled as he saw the sheriff enter the small building. He stood and reached his hand. Mikhail took it.

"Morning, Sheriff. What brings you to my little office?"

"Trouble, Robert."

"I heard about the cattle driver. Damn shame. Didn't know the man myself but Marie said he was good man." He flushed as he mentioned Marie.

"Tracey is dead, as well."

Robert's face went pale. "No. How?"

"Killed in her sleep. We are gathering up at the jail to search the town for the killer."

"It wasn't one of us, was it?"

There were only fourteen people, thirteen now Mikhail corrected himself, that lived in the small town. Village, really. Community if he were being honest. There was another thirty or so that lived outside of the town on farmsteads. After the town was searched, he would need to ride out and check on them. After he knew Jia-Li was safe.

"I doubt it. Whatever did it was not human. It was

pure evil." He filled Robert in on the details. The postal clerk's hands trembled as he listened. He was another former soldier and had seen his share of atrocities. But enemy combatants were one thing. A lady everyone had dealings with was another completely.

"I have my shotgun and rifle ready as always. Let me gather some ammo and my pistols and I'll be there shortly."

"I thank you kindly, Robert. Karl will be leading us. He has the most experience in these affairs. Consider him lawfully deputized. I need to check on River and Hasse now, but I'll be there in a bit."

"They ain't there, sheriff. I heard an awful commotion last night carry through the dark. Then I heard the sound of hooves headed out. By the time I had gotten up and peeked out the window, there was a cloud of dust headed West. I suspect toward the tribes."

Mikhail frowned. What could have been so pressing as to send them out in the middle of the night? He didn't believe the words, but Teddy's admonitions echoed in his head. No. There was no chance of that. But it was mighty peculiar.

"You ready, Sheriff?" Robert stood with his guns at the door.

"Let's get this over with."

Josiah and Teddy walked with a purpose into the church as if prepared to rain down judgment on any creature that dared accost them or their town. Once inside, all pretense went out the window.

"Those God damned savages done it!" Teddy yelled.

Josiah nodded sagely. "They are a scourge upon the land. But you cannot convince the idiots that live here of their evil intent. They are so blinded by the falsehoods they cannot see what is so clearly in front of them. They will see the truth of it."

"Sheriff wants us to head to the jail and meet up with that Beck character. I don't trust him. Not one bit. He stinks of the big cities. Highfalutin know-it-alls, the whole bunch of them."

"What the Sheriff wants and what God wants are two different things. Come on, Teddy, the Lord willed it so that I have a bottle stashed away in the back. Perhaps a sip or two will calm our moods. The rest can wait."

Teddy licked his lips and nodded. There was not a time he didn't think a nip or two was the best suggestion. He followed Josiah to the pulpit and made note of the loose board at the bottom. Josiah lifted out a half full bottle of rye and held it out to Teddy who tried not to seem too eager. He pulled the cork with his teeth and took a moderate drink before passing back.

"Dear Jesus, I beseech thee to smite down the Savages that have slain poor Tracey Wilson and returned her to your embrace. Protect the foolhardy men of this small town as well in their fruitless search for demons. Open their eyes to the true evil. In your name we pray and give thanks. Amen."

Teddy echoed the amen. But he kept waiting for Josiah to take a drink and pass it back. Finally, Josiah took a drink but he kept the bottle. Teddy seethed as he watched the amber liquid in the bottle. He didn't want to hear another speech. He wanted another sip.

"The Lord will provide for us, dear Teddy. We are the only members of this flock that truly do His work. We shall be repaid in heaven with vast rewards!"

Teddy stared at the bottle, hoping to encourage him to drink instead of talk. Then he saw something drip down onto the sleeve of Josiah's jacket. Rain? No. The sky was clear when they walked in, he remembered. Another drop hit the preacher's jacket. This time it splashed a bit on to the pulpit. Teddy blinked his eyes as he looked at it. It almost seemed red in the dim light streaming through the dusty windows.

"Yes, my friend, the Lord shall bring is into his bosom as heroes and true believers. You mark my words! When we die, our lives will just have begun!"

Another drop splashed and Josiah at last noticed. He touched his sleeve and looked at his finger in bewilderment. Then he looked at Teddy who was staring up at the rafters with a slack jaw and pale face. Then the smell hit him and he moved to cover his mouth from the rancid odor. He looked up as well and saw the Devil with gray skin crouched on the bare wood grinning down at them. In its hands was a half-eaten . . . was that a dog? The thing just smiled down at them. Then it dropped the grisly snack and fell silently onto its feet in front of them.

Teddy snatched the bottle from Josiah's hand and took a long gulp, draining a quarter of the bottle as Josiah just sputtered. The thing walked toward them, still grinning wide with blood flecked teeth and dead, black eyes. Josiah made the mark of the cross to ward off evil as Teddy drained the remains of the rye.

It leaned forward and snarled, *"Pleeeeease cooooooooome untoooooooo meeeeeeeee."*

Teddy threw the bottle and the creature snatched it out of the air and brought it down against the pulpit with a shattering sound. Josiah opened his mouth to yell but was cut off as the broken bottle was thrust into his throat. All that came out was a wet gurgle. Teddy made a move to run as Josiah clutched the mouth of the bottle. Blood poured out in gouts from the makeshift spout. The creature grabbed Josiah by the right arm and wrenched his arm off of his body and slammed it into Teddy's back midstride with enough force to knock him off of his feet. Josiah stared with no comprehension that he was dead for a long moment before slumping to the floor in a pool of his own blood.

Teddy got to his knees as the monster landed on his back. The breath left his body at the jarring impact and he wheezed as he felt ribs crack. The long gray claws raked down his back, all the way down to the bone. He would have screamed if he could draw enough breath. The world took on a red tinge as agony assaulted his brain and he felt consciousness begin to slip away. Then the evil incarnate reached into the bloody, tattered flesh and gripped his spine and ripped it out with a grunt of exertion and triumph. It held it up to its snarling lips and ran a long blackish tongue across the vertebrae, savoring the taste of spinal fluid and blood.

"Soooooooooooooon, Haaaaaaaaaaaaaaseeeeeeeee eeee"

River stood, tension and fear barely concealed. He was a compressed spring waiting to fly into a fit of rage. Hasse Ola lay on the ground before the great fire. His every muscle rigid, white-lipped with a low moan sounding through clenched teeth.

"We must perform the ceremony this evening." All eyes faced the speaker, the Muscogee chief, as he pleaded with the others.

"We are not prepared. And the moon is not either."

"Damn your excuses!" River shouted. "All you have done for the last decades is talk while we have lost everything! It is time for action. This boy needs you."

"Your time with the White Man has cost you your patience. Their ways are not ours, our ways are not theirs."

River spat on the ground. "Soon all will be theirs. As you sit and talk of our ways, the world outside changes. You collect dust across your still forms and call it tradition."

"Enough. What we propose is dangerous enough for not only the boy, but all of us as well. It is not to be taken lightly. The sacred ceremonies must be honored. If you cannot, then slit his throat instead. If you wish him saved, stop your tongue."

River glared at the fire but was quiet.

Hasse Ola screamed loud into the tent, a primal sound of pain and torment that made even the most stoic of the tribesmen flinch.

"All in favor of proceeding?"

Slowly, all raised a hand into the air, even if their faces showed great distaste and doubt.

"Then tonight we shall perform the rites. Until then, cleanse yourselves. We must be purified for this to work, mind and spirit."

"Where in Hell are the preacher and the drunkard?" Mikhail seemed beside himself with anger.

Bradley sat quietly. Cody was looking through one of the journals on the table with wide eyes. It was obvious he had a thousand questions he wanted ask. But the expression on Karl's face kept him silent. Robert stood ready for action, watching out the window at the empty street.

"I have nothing. Not a single damned thing." Karl pushed the last sheaf of paper away in disgust. He slammed his fist onto the table.

"What do we do?" Mikhail stood with his hand on his revolver.

"Duncan isn't all that big, really. Just the strip besides all the farmhouses. I get the feeling the creature is still here, though. If it went to the outskirts, everyone would already be dead. This is a hunter. It relishes fear. The way it posted her head tells me it wants us to be afraid of what it is capable of doing. We split up into two groups and each take one side of the street. Search barns and hay with pitchforks. Jam then into the loose hay, it may be waiting under cover. It may be nocturnal like a vampyre or revenant. Chances are it is resilient and fast. Teeth and claws, most likely."

"I've seen some tough bastards in my life, ain't a one of them been able to take buckshot to the belly, though." Bradley put on a heavy dose of bravado, but all of the men radiated apprehensive fear.

"Sheriff, you take Robert and Cody. I'll go with Bradley and his buckshot. Go slow, be careful. It knows we are here but may not be aware we know it is. Most monsters will seek some place they can defend in the presence of men. Our ignorance is against us. We need to hope its ignorance is against it as well."

The men walked to the door and stopped as they saw the telltale cloud of dust signal a rider coming into town fast. They watched the rider draw closer and Robert said, "It is River coming back from the tribes, I reckon. Looks to be alone as well."

River heeled his horse, both covered in a sheen of sweat and hopped off. "Sheriff, greetings."

Mikhail eyed him for a moment before speaking. The words of Teddy ringing in his head. "We had a spell of trouble last night here in town. A cattle driver showed up mighty injured and passed. This morning we found Tracey killed as well. I went to warn you but seems you and Hasse bolted in the middle of the night."

"How were they killed?"

"Chris was attacked and snake bit. Tracey was partially consumed." Karl watched River's expression and saw no shock register. "Now, usually when I tell someone another person has been eaten, they look disgusted and upset. You don't seem to be either. Care to explain?"

River's shoulders slumped. "Hasse Ola took sick last night. But not before he spoke."

The men of Duncan looked as if they had been struck.

"The boy ain't dumb?" Bradley asked in surprise. He looked at the others. "I thought he couldn't talk. I ain't heard a word in the two years we've been here."

Cody shrugged as he studied the horse with an intent expression. Mikhail and Karl just waited for River to continue.

"He said one word before he passed out." He stared at the dirt road. Karl felt himself biting his tongue to keep from screaming. "Wendigo."

Karl stared at him with a stupefied expression. "Wendigo? Impossible. They don't ever leave the wilds of Western Canada."

River looked at him with a grin devoid of mirth. "There are many myths among the Peoples. As varied as the tribes themselves. The Algonquin legends and the Muscogee tales."

Karl nodded but his expression showed frustration. "I'm aware of the different mythos between tribes. I have also spent significant time with the Muscogee Tribe. I never once heard their version of the Wendigo. What are their weaknesses? What drives them? What does this have to do with Hasse Ola?"

River frowned. "They are not my people. Although I look at Hasse Ola as a younger brother, he is not blood of my blood. I have cared for him these last three years. He was there, three years ago when the Miller Gang was slaughtered on the Chisholm Trail. He had been taken by the outlaw scum and was about to be tortured for information on some sort of treasure they searched for."

"What treasure?" Bradley suddenly seemed a lot more interested in the mumbo jumbo he had found himself tuning out.

River spat. "A myth, nothing more. Something locked away far to the South of here. But the outlaws didn't know anything about that. They had him strung up to a tree when the Wendigo found them. He killed them all except for Hasse Ola."

"Why did it spare the boy?" Mikhail questioned.

"The Elders never spoke of why he was not killed. They are careful with their words, more so when it is an outsider asking. All they would say is the Wendigo is a hunter driven by hunger and greed."

"And its weakness?" Karl prodded.

"They never said. I never asked. They were convinced it was long dead. Or left far behind as we were pushed farther and farther from home."

Guilty looks filled the faces of the men listening. All except for Cody who was still staring at the horse and mumbling to himself.

"So, we finally know what it is," Mikhail muttered.

"But we have no clue how to stop it," Karl added. "And it is here in town waiting for us. Somewhere."

"Are you sticking around to help us, River? Or you got to get back to the tribes?" Mikhail stared at him as he asked. There seemed little doubt as to which he preferred.

"I fear this evil is threaded into Hasse Ola's spirit. If we can destroy it, he will be free. I freely lend my help to you."

"You're with Karl, then. No stone left unturned, gentlemen. We find this sonovabitch, we end it, then everything goes back to peaceful times."

"Except for Chris and Tracey. And Lord knows how many others that is," Robert added.

"We avenge the fallen. And maybe save Hasse Ola, as well. Let's go."

The two groups of men nodded and headed to the opposite sides of the quiet main street. Grim determination drove them as their boots stomped along the hard-packed ground, fear in their bellies as they searched for the Devil hidden somewhere in Duncan.

Hours passed as the six men combed through every hay bale and empty room of town. The sun had sat high in the sky when they began, but now cast angry red across the town as they reached the church. It had been fruitless. There was no sign of hide nor hair of any monsters to be found. To the East, the coyotes cried as the darkness grew heavy across half the sky.

Mikhail looked at Karl and shook his head in disappointment. "Not a damned thing to be found. I'm guessing by the looks on your faces the same holds true for you as well?"

Karl stared dejectedly at the ground. "Perhaps it got what it wanted and left. All that is left is to tell the drunks in the church and go to Kenzie's for some grub."

Brad spit a fat spray of brown tobacco juice out. "Those two chickenshits never did come out of their little hiding spot to help us. Bet they holed up with some whiskey and waited until we done all the searchin'."

"Well let's roust the lazy sacks of shit and get a well-deserved meal. The ladies are probably plum scared out their minds waiting for us." Robert blushed as he spoke, and smiles greeted his words as everyone knew exactly which lady he was worried about.

Mikhail kicked the closed double doors of the church. "Alright you lily-livered bastards. You can come out now!" He kicked the door again. "Probably passed out. Teddy and Josiah both don't know when to quit drinkin'."

Karl reached for the door and then stopped. "You hear that?"

Everyone grew quiet for a moment and heard a loud buzzing sound. They looked confusedly at each other.

"Sounds like flies. A whole heap of flies," Cody said quietly.

Karl pulled his rifle off of his back and cocked back the hammer and held it ready. He looked at Mikhail and nodded. Mikhail reached forward and grabbed the doorknob. The rest of the men had their weapons drawn and at the ready. Mikhail signaled with three fingers. Two. One. Then he turned and pushed as he dropped to a knee beneath Karl's line of sight.

The stench hit them like a wave and they all cringed. The red light filtered in as Karl made his way slowly in. He froze less than five steps in, then began to aim down the long barrel as he checked the corners of the building. No stranger to monsters, he also sighted along the rafters. He felt nauseated as he looked around the now defiled room. The stench of death and thick clouds of flies filled the air. Bradley stepped in and then quickly turned back and made loud retching noises outside. Karl couldn't blame him. He reached into his pocket and pulled out a few matches. He struck one across his zipper and the sulphur filled his nostril as the light flared.

"My God in heaven," Mikhail muttered.

Cody stared in disgusted awe at the scene in front of them as Karl lit a couple candles. Teddy was laid out across the large wooden cross in the back of the room. Not laid out precisely. Strewn. His head was impaled on the top of it. Fragments of shattered skull and reddish gray chunks of flesh hung limply. It looked more like a watermelon had been thrust down on the wood than a man's head. His face was sagging and both eyes had been removed. His tongue hung on his pallid, blood splashed chin. Somehow his torso was affixed to the main post of the cross just beneath the intersecting beam. His ropy intestines hung down to spool onto the floor. Great clouds of flies swarmed around him.

Bradley remained outside vomiting, the stench too much for him to even consider coming inside to see the cause of it. Mikhail and Karl slowly made their way to the cross with weapons at the ready. Cody couldn't take his eyes off of the remains. "Where are his arms and legs?" he asked softly. "And where is Josiah?"

Karl didn't say a word as he made his way forward. The wooden floor was covered in blood. His boots made an off-putting sucking sound as he walked. Mikhail kept pace just behind him. They searched the pulpit area and behind the desecrated cross.

Mikhail broke the silence finally. "How could any creature do this?"

Karl walked behind the cross and let out a low whistle. "It ripped out his spine. Tore it clean out of his body and then jammed the remains on the cross itself. This is the Wendigo taunting us. A show of power and savagery."

"It ripped out his spine?" Cody's eyes lit up at the prospect of seeing that.

His scientific curiosity mixed with the mushrooms he had consumed right before the sheriff found him sent his mind into a whirlwind. He hurried forward to see and slipped in the thick blood and fell onto his back with a jarring thud and splash. He lay in the syrupy pool and tried to catch his breath. He stared up to the rafters and swore he felt eyes staring back down on him. He blinked and kept looking but all he saw was darkness. Then he saw a faint flicker of motion. He opened his mouth to speak but realized he didn't know if what he was seeing was actually there to be seen or not. He had sworn that River's horse was trying to give him a message earlier. He turned his head and saw River standing there with a hand out to help him up, which he gladly took, all while refraining from looking up into the dark above him.

"Thanks, River. I appreciate it."

River stared at him. "You are covered in blood. Why were you just laying in it?"

Cody opened his mouth to speak when he saw the darkness drop from the rafters and land behind River soundlessly. His mouth moved but no words exited it, just a primal groan which was barely enough of a sign. River crouched quickly and a gray skinned arm swung where his head had just been. He spun and fired his gun twice at near point-blank range. A spray of black ichor rained against the back wall.

The entire church exploded into a cacophony of gunfire. The Wendigo was hit and torn by the bullets, driven back against the wall where it snarled in rage before sliding down to sit motionless. The men stopped shooting and stared at it. Lean and covered in deep scars and black oozing holes along its corded, wiry frame. The gray skin hung in flaps from where the hot lead tore through it.

Bradley still looked green but he stared at the creature from the doorway. "That wasn't so bad for a demon from the depths of Hell."

Karl didn't move and when Mikhail stepped forward to examine the body, he held out a hand to stop him. "Not yet. I'm not convinced it isn't playing possum."

Mikhail laughed. "Ain't no possum alive can survive that many bullets."

"We may have seen distinctly different possums in our time."

Cody was in awe of the thing. "Do you realize the kind of discovery for science this is? Monsters have always been tall tales told to explain the incomprehensible fear of the dark. But here lies the corpse of one. I need to dissect it. Learn from it. Who knows what secrets it may hide? New discoveries that will further our understanding of the world we live in."

He held his gun out and began to approach the Wendigo. His mind was already running through the possibilities. He would be famous. Perhaps land a teaching job at one of the schools back East. He was so caught up in thought he didn't hear the warnings from Karl to stop. The stench of rot was so strong he felt his eyes watering. Bullets had penetrated the chest and lungs. He reached out and grabbed the wrist of the creature and felt for a pulse, but his excitement was so strong all he felt was his own pounding in his chest and skull. He was vibrating. He pulled put his long sharp blade from its sheath on his belt and held it beneath the creature's nose. "No sign of fogging. No sign of a pulse. Gentlemen, I believe we have ended the Wendigo's reign of terror."

Karl kept watching in anticipation. In his mind, he was counting down. How many times had a creature fallen only to get back up at the last minute? He had scars to show what overconfidence could do. But it didn't shift at all. Just stayed hunched down against the wall with blood dripping from its wounds. He found himself smiling in amazement.

Mikhail saw his smile and slapped him on the shoulder. "Looks like the big bad Wendigo couldn't stand up to Sheriff Mikhail and his deputies. I imagine this will be a story you will tell to your grandchildren. Make sure to mention my fearlessness in the face of peril. And my rugged good looks."

"Leave out the part about me puking my guts out," Bradley called as he walked back out into the dusk.

"What do you want done with the body?" Karl asked River. "He was clearly once one of the Tribes."

Cody stood and faced River. "I need to study it. For all of mankind."

River stared at the corpse and shrugged. "It is an abomination and no part of the Tribes any longer. Let sawbones do as he will."

Cody smiled and nodded. "Yes, yes. Thank you. If you could help me get it across the street to my office. I want to start the autopsy immediately."

"I can save you time and effort, Cody. It died of lead poisoning." Mikhail laughed and soon the rest of the men joined him.

River bent down and grabbed the Wendigo by the legs and nodded to Cody who grabbed its arms. They lifted it with a grunt and left the church.

"Let's go let the ladies know we have vanquished the foul beast and grab some of Ms. Kenzie's cooking. Possibly a bottle or five of whiskey as well," Mikhail said as he moved towards the door.

"What about all of this?" Karl pointed at Teddy still hanging limply from the cross.

"I'm thinking a fire is in order. This place will never be clean again. Burn it to the ground and start fresh again when the new sheriff gets to town."

"And Josiah?"

"He'll turn up. One way or another."

Bradley was nothing but smiles as Karl closed the door behind him. "Whiskey and dinner is on me, boys! And maybe I'll get lucky and Mary Jo hasn't left yet."

"You like that foul-mouthed artist?" Robert asked with a smile.

"She makes purdy paintings. Knows her way around a brush, if'n you catch my meaning. I'm sure you and Marie haven't gotten there quite yet. You two being civilized folk and all."

The men laughed and walked as Robert's face flared red in the fading light.

River helped Cody dump the body on the examination table and turned to leave.

"Where you headed? There's gonna be a party tonight at Kenzie's. I'm going to start my investigation and head over myself soon."

HUNGER ON THE CHISHOLM TRAIL

"I need to tell the Chiefs what went down. That the Wendigo is dead. Hasse Ola has his ceremony this evening, as well. If I hurry, I can make it for the end if it. We shall celebrate as well. A great evil was ended this evening, one that carried a heavy burden over my people. The people of Duncan shall be remembered for this." With that, he went outside the office.

Cody leaned his head out the doorway. "See if you can get more of those mushrooms while you are there!"

River laughed and continued down the street.

Cody returned to the office table and shrugged out of his heavy, bloodstained clothes. He went out the back door and pumped a basin of water and washed as much of the sticky red mess off as possible. He was dripping as he grabbed one of the towels off the shelf and dried himself. His mind was still racing at the thought of a book and tour. Maybe head to Europe with the specimens. He dressed into the change of clothes he always left in the bottom of his desk and shrugged on a rough spun long coat to keep himself clean.

He returned to the Wendigo with an ink pot and pen to journal his discoveries.

Of Men and Monsters, Hunger on the Chisholm Trail, he began. He wrote out the story of Hasse Ola and Tracey in quick efficient handwriting. Then he told the tale of Chris lashed over the back of a horse brought into town with stories of the Devil on the trail. He smiled as he read his words back. The fading effects of the mushrooms still lent a dreamlike quality to his words. He made a note to ask Karl about other monsters. Maybe he could go along on an adventure with him? This was just the beginning of his rise to fame. He could tell. He knew when he headed out to the middle of nowhere, he was destined for greatness. No one in the cities believed in him. But here he was allowed to do things his way.

He set down his paper and moved to look over the thing that would elevate his practice. He stared at the body in wonder. The skin shade was unusual, perhaps a freak pigmentation like albinism. He reached forward and peeled up an eyelid and was amazed at the all black orbs. He wished Duncan had a photographer. He imagined there would be one soon, once word of this being home to a monster spread. People could not contain themselves when given a glimpse into the dark.

He turned and grabbed a Mason jar from the shelf and the large bottle of formaldehyde as well. He mixed a healthy amount of formaldehyde into the jar and added alcohol to fill it near the top. He turned back to the body with a small knife to try and carefully pluck the eyes out. The all black would make onlookers shiver in fright, he told himself with a grin.

"That's peculiar," he muttered as he saw the eye had closed again. He chuckled to himself at the momentary spike of adrenaline he felt. "Rigor Mortis may be settling in causing the muscle to spasm and shutting the eye."

Then he noticed something else strange. The bullet wounds seemed to be knitting themselves back together before his eyes. He blinked a few times, blaming it on hallucinations. No. As he watched the body, it mended itself. He watched in fascination as realization dawned upon him. The thing was still alive. He turned to run out of the room but felt a hand snap up and grab him by the arm. He was wrenched back to the table and found himself staring into those inky eyes filled with malice and hunger.

"Doooooooooooooon'tttttt ruuuuuuuuun."

"Please don't kill me. Please. I'm begging you," Cody groveled.

The Wendigo just smiled at him, a cold smile devoid of anything remotely human. Then its other hand flew forward into his face. Cody felt his eyes rupture and ocular jelly run down his face. That was the last sensation he felt as the claws broke through the thin layer of skull and into his brain. His body jerked as the electrical impulses raced in a state of confusion through him. He was no longer there as the teeth began to rip into his cheek.

The office was filled with sounds of cracking bones and wet smacking as the Wendigo feasted upon Cody. A splatter of blood flew across the room and stained the pages of his magnum opus and soaked through the paper.

13

THE TRIBES

THE SUNSET LEFT only the faintest light on the far horizon. The men returned from the hunt with haunches of fresh meat slung over the back of their horses. Campfires dotted the area as dinners cooked and tendrils of smoke rose lazily into the sky. The makeshift town was lively and filled with smiles, the hustle of the day giving in to the peace of the evening.

The Medicine Lodge was hushed as the chiefs filed in. Each brought an offering of sage and hide to appease the spirits. They solemnly bowed their heads before the blazing fire and made peace with the ancestors that watched over them. The gifts were consumed, and the smoke felt heavy as it drifted up through vents in the canopy.

The chief of the Muscogee, now one of equals among the Tribes, sat singing gently as he ground the sacred dyes. He took long pulls from the water skin filled with berries and herbs that had been left to ferment for weeks. He spit into the dyes as he crushed and mixed them together. At his side, a young hunter that had been chosen to learn the secrets of Medicine from the elders and ancestors sat sharpening branches into fine points.

Hasse Ola had sat still for the last hour. His fever seemed on the verge of breaking. The ropes around his arms and legs relaxed along with his taut muscles that had been at the point of tearing the last cycle of sun and moon. He was still bound, tethered with arms above his head to stakes driven into the soil. But his face carried a sense of serenity. Each chief sang softly the songs of his people as they waved sage over the still form.

Hasse Ola opened his eyes and looked around with confusion faint in the brown orbs. One of the chiefs held a skin to his lips and let water trickle into his mouth. He sighed contentedly and his eyelids slid closed again.

"He has relaxed. The spirits hear our pleas. Let the ritual begin."

14

KENZIE'S

WHEN THE FOUR MEN entered the bar, seven sets of eyes met them with looks of hope and anxiety. Jia-Li ran to Mikhail and wrapped him in a bear hug. Marie was on her heels and grabbed Robert's face and pulled him down to plant a fierce kiss on his lips. The ladies hooted and hollered at the display. Robert stood stiff as a board for a moment and it was obvious he was a mixture of shocked and embarrassed at first. But, eventually the passion swept through him and he gave as good as he received.

Bradley stopped in the doorway and Kenzie gave him a smile. Then his head snapped to the side. Mary Jo stood glaring daggers at him. "What in tarnation was that for?" he demanded.

"You are an idjit. Do you hear me, Bradley? An idjit. What were you thinking? You could have woken me up, I'm a sight better shooting than you, I reckon. What if you'd been injured?"

He stared at her in confusion. "You told me you

162

were leaving town to take the horse back as soon as you got up. How in the hell was I supposed to . . . " His head snapped to the other side. He looked at the outlaw in bewilderment.

She stared at him with equal disapproval. "Ain't as if you argued. Or offered to ride with me."

He was thoroughly confused now. "Did you want me to?"

Her face softened. "I wouldn't say no. That's for sure."

"Did you wait for me?"

"I ain't no fool. If'n there was a monster loose out there, I'd make a soft target for it."

He reached out and grabbed her hand. It was both a gesture of affection and to prevent a third slap. "Darling, there ain't nothing soft about you. Well, some soft bits, I reckon. But I like them too." He pulled her in and kissed her gently on the lips. The ladies hollered nearly as loudly as they had for Marie.

Kenzie cringed a bit, probably debating if she just lost a good partner or gained an awful one. Karl smiled sadly at the happy faces, his mind on Tracey and the date that was never to be. He approached the bar and Kenzie rested her hand on his shoulder and gave him a sweet smile that reflected pain in his eyes. He nodded to her, words seemingly stuck in his throat and took the offered glass of whiskey she held out to him.

Frank and Otto, the two travelers, sat watching the spectacle. Frank seemed confused by the ordeal. Otto was indifferently staring with his lips down in a frown.

Kenzie watched as Karl sipped the drink slowly.

When he finally set the glass down, she spoke. "I'm taking it you got the bastard?"

"That we did."

"Did we lose anyone else?"

"Teddy. And we didn't find Josiah anywhere." Everyone grew quiet as he told the tale of the scene in the church. He relayed River's words as well. When he finished speaking, silence filled the room.

"Bullshit," Frank exclaimed as the silence lingered. Otto set his hand on his friend's arm, but Frank shrugged it off. "No. That is the biggest load of cockamamie I have heard. A gray skinned savage done up and killed Lord knows how many people. And ate them too? Horse shit."

Robert took an angry step toward the men, but Marie placed a hand on his chest. Mikhail cast an angry stare from over his wife's head.

It was Mary Jo that spun in a fit of anger, her hands resting in her weapons. "Listen to me, coward, and listen good. Don't think I didn't see the both of ya nearly piss your drawers when you found out what was happenin'. It took Ms. Jia-Li and Ms. Kenzie to hold me back. But the two of you no good, lousy mongrels didn't lift finger one nor offer your assistance. Now you remember your balls when the killin' is done. I've a mind to put you down myself. Lily-livered cowards."

Otto held up his hands. "Listen, ma'am, Frank here is just drunk and talking out of his backside. It's just we ain't never heard of one of those windmill-go things. Please accept our apologies. And our thanks. Ain't that right, Frank?"

Frank muttered something into his glass and Otto

slapped him upside the head. "My apologies, ma'am. Gentlemen. I've been in the cups all day and don't rightly know what I'm sayin'."

Bradley pulled Mary Jo back and wrapped his arms around her front. "Thank you, darling."

She melted back into him and sighed. The storm had passed and everyone returned to chatting. Marie led Robert to the bar and pulled out his stool. He sat and took the glass of whiskey. Then she sat down on his lap and rested her head against his chest.

Mikhail and Jia-Li walked over and sat by Karl. "Thank you for bringing my pup back to me unharmed, Mr. Beck."

Karl smiled at her. "My pleasure. Hell of a man you have there."

She patted Mikhail's cheek and smiled at him while wrinkling her nose. "The best. And quite pretty too, even though he smells like a slaughterhouse."

They all sat and drank while Bradley told the same story they had just heard but managed to embellish every detail. Soon, the Wendigo was twelve-foot-tall and he stared up at it with a crooked grin and unleashed fire upon it. Mikhail gave a glance at Karl and both men burst out laughing.

"You've got a bit of vomit on your trousers and boots, Bradley," Kenzie called out as he was singlehandedly taking the creature down. Everyone burst into fresh laughter as he flushed and hurriedly looked down.

For that moment, all was right in Duncan. Every single person was smiling and drinking. Even Frank and Otto seemed to be relaxed as they took it all in. Outside, the old owl let out a hoot and flew past the lively bar on its rounds to find a rabbit for its breakfast. Peace seemed to settle over the town like a blanket.

Then it went to hell.

The front window of the bar shattered inwards and Tara and Amber let out screams. The projectile that broke the window landed with a thud and rolled to rest at Frank's boots. He looked down at it and fell backward out of his chair.

Josiah's head stared at the ceiling with a grisly look of shock.

"Pleeeeease   dooooooooooooon'tttttt" came howling from the street outside.

Karl leapt off of his stool with his weapon drawn. Mikhail was up at the same time. Karl looked at Bradley. "Get the women in the back room."

"What the hell is that out there? The Wendigo is dead." Kenzie couldn't take her eyes off of Josiah's head.

As if to answer, the other window exploded inwards. Cody's head landed on a table next to the bar. The gaping holes where the eyes once were and flesh eaten off of the cheeks caused no shortage of screaming as Bradley ushered the women out of the room. Mary Jo shrugged him off, as did Jia-Li.

"We stay."

"Baby, go. Please. This thing took at least ten shots and we were sure it was dead."

"You don't shoot as well as I do."

"I can't lose you."

"You won't."

"Cooooooooome unnnnnnnntoooo meeeeeeeee"

Mary Jo fired a few shots out the broken window.

"Come and get me, you shit heel!" She stomped out the front door. Karl followed her. Mikhail and Jia-Li stood staring out into the street through the empty window frames.

"It is a hunter. Be wary." Karl cautioned her.

"I shot the balls off of a gopher once at fifty yards. I ain't scared of no gray skinned freak."

"I don't doubt your skill. But this thing is a killer."

"Well, I ain't been killed yet. And I've faced down some real bastards."

"I reckon you have."

No sooner did the words leave his mouth then a black streak, darkness on darkness flew in front of him. One moment Mary Jo was there, the next her legs and boots were spurting blood onto the street. He heard her scream in the distance and gunfire. He stood in shock staring at the boots as they fell over. Mikhail was suddenly there and pulled him back into the bar.

"It moved so fast." Karl still stared in shock out at the street. "I never saw it coming."

Mikhail and Jia-Li steered him to the back room and slammed the door behind them.

"Where's Mary Jo?" Bradley asked. Karl stared at him. Jia-Li and Mikhail looked at the floor. "Where is she?"

"Gone. It happened so fast. I couldn't do anything. She's gone, Bradley."

Bradley made a noise of rage that seemed to vibrate from his very soul. He grabbed his shotgun and made for the door. Mikhail grabbed his shoulder but he shrugged it off. Kenzie cried out but he ignored her and walked out the door. Mikhail went to follow but Karl stopped him.

"I'll go. Get everyone upstairs. It is fast but I doubt it can fly. Lock yourselves into the rooms."

"Then I'm going, too."

Karl saw the look on Jia-Li's face and he patted Mikhail on the shoulder. "No. I've got this. Keep everyone safe until I get back. It wants us to chase after it."

"Then why are you doing it?"

"Because it isn't the first thing to want me to chase it. I don't die here, not like this. Trust me."

And he walked out the open door.

15

THE TRIBES

THE **GATHERING OF** chiefs danced around the fire, their songs filling the tent and spilling out into the night. The stars above seemed to pulse and fade with the cadence of their singing. They tossed powders onto the flames and colors sparked into life. A hush had fallen over the tents outside as the effects of powerful magic sent reverberations through the air.

Hasse Ola twitched as the ink laden sticks broke his skin. The beginning of intricate patterns took form upon his bleeding chest and stomach. Wards against evil carefully etched from memory, passed down from generation to generation, infused with holy protection. As the song built in power around him, he began to thrash more and more. It was as if the evil had already tried to desperately take root in his body and mind and fought against the ritual. Hours remained until it was all complete, but the faces around wore grim determination.

His head thrust back and his entire body

tightened. He let a bellow of anguish and rage into the tent that made the song falter slightly. It resumed with even more power as he screamed. His eyes snapped open and stared malevolently at the hides above him. His left eye pained, brown with a pupil as small as the tip of the wooden needle. His right eye all black filled with hatred and hunger.

Bradley stood in the street, staring at the boots laying on their sides in two pools of blood. Tears ran freely down his cheeks as he clenched the shotgun with white knuckles.

"Get back here, you dumb son of a bitch," Karl whispered, watching the shadows.

Bradley didn't move a muscle. He stood frozen.

"Bradley. C'mon, snap out of it. Getting your damned fool ass killed doesn't bring her back."

He turned and faced Karl. "Why? What did we ever do to this thing? What did she ever do except get drunk and paint?"

Karl put an arm around his shoulders and guided him back to the bar. "They don't think the same as us. They are driven by need. Evil isn't bound to the same rules as we are. Let's go back inside where it's safe, alright?"

"We gotta make it pay, Karl. For Cody and Mary Jo. And Tracey, too." He began sobbing against Karl's shoulder. Karl awkwardly patted his back while trying to stare in every direction at once.

"We will. Let's go inside. We are exposed out here. Close quarters will be best. You head inside. Everyone is upstairs. Go and lock yourself in with Kenzie. She needs you now."

Bradley stood taller and wiped his face with his sleeve. He tried to center himself and walked back into the bar. Karl smiled at him encouragingly. Then he turned back to the street.

"I'm right here, you mangy bastard! Come out and face me!" he shouted into the night.

"*Iiiiiiiiiiiiiiiiiiiiiii'mmmmmm heeeeeeeeeeerrrr eeeeeee.*"

Karl whipped around to find the source of the voice. His jaw dropped as Bradley turned toward him, mouth moving soundlessly. As he watched, it was as if Bradley came apart at the seams. He stood pale faced with his lips moving and his intestines and guts poured out in a rush of blood and viscera onto the bar floor in a torrent. Bradley stared down at the floor as he tried to comprehend what was happening. He desperately reached down to pull the bloody ropes back into the now empty cavity. He fell to his knees in slow motion. Karl couldn't blink or convince himself to move. He watched as the Wendigo smiled, darkness against the dark. It swiped one claw casually and Bradley's head tumbled off his still moving corpse. It stared at Karl for a long second, the grin never fading, and then turned and ran for the stairs.

"Mikhail! It's coming up the stairs!" he shouted. He saw the curtains flutter above him. He forced himself to move, his body fighting against him. His mind screaming to get on a horse and ride as fast and as far away as possible. Instead, he began to run inside, screaming warning to those upstairs.

The screaming began as he reached the bottom of

the stairs, soon followed by gunfire. He took the stairs two at a time and ran through the splintered doorway into the bedroom. It had been seconds. Ten. Maybe fifteen. But that was all it had taken for Tara to have been slit from inner thigh to throat. She lay gasping on the bed as her life drained into the feather stuffed mattress. Amber was sticking out of the wall. Literally. Her cotton stocking covered legs twitched. Her arms were pinned to her sides as she had been forcefully thrust through the wall. Her Derringer still clutched in her hand.

"Amber, are you still alive?" he asked. Sounds of gunfire came from the opposite side of where she has been rammed.

"Help me, Karl! My face is broken and I am stuck. I'm bleedin' bad. Please get me out of this. I'm . . . "

"Amber!" Karl pulled on her legs to free her. He tugged and she began to scream. "I've got you! Just a little mo . . . "

He fell backwards with her in his arms on the floor. The wind knocked out of his chest and his head cracked the floor hard enough to send sparks across his vision. He lay there dizzily for a moment still clutching her thighs. Gunfire rang throughout the building. He shook the cobwebs out of his head and looked down to see how she was faring. He felt bile surge into his mouth as he saw he held onto half of her. He turned his head and vomited on the faux Oriental rug that was already saturated with Tara's blood and kicked the half body off of his legs. He staggered to his feet and stared through the hole in the wall. The Wendigo was there stalking towards Bella. Kenzie lay crumpled in a broken heap, her head turned sickeningly too far to the left

"Per favore, Dio no! Per favore abbi Pietà!" she cried.

Karl shot through the hole in the wooden timbers. The Wendigo shook as each bullet hit but continued moving forward. Karl fired again and again until the hammer clicked on an empty chamber. He tossed the gun and pulled his other and saw the creature raise its lean, muscled arms with long jagged claws into the air. Karl murmured a prayer and fired once more. The creature screamed out a bellow of unbridled fury as the bullet slammed through Bella's eye. Karl felt hollow in his action but knew he gave her a quick death. A faint bit of mercy at best that tasted like ashes when mixed with his failure.

"Yoooooooooou'rrrrrrrrreeee laaaaaaaaaaaasss sssssst," the Wendigo hissed in rage at him. Then it leapt forward into the sturdy wall in front of it and crashed through like it was made if rice paper.

Marie screamed in terror and the sound of a double barrel percussion exploded. Robert was yelling incoherently. Karl ran toward the door, then found himself falling face first onto the floor with a crunch as his nose was broken. His feet had gotten tangled up in Amber's legs and tripped him up. He would have laughed at the black horror of it all, but he could barely breathe. His eyes were watering as he pulled himself up and staggered into the hallway in time to see Robert's body thrown over the railing of the landing to land with a crash as it hit the wall of liquor behind the bar.

Karl looked over the railing and saw Robert was not going to be getting up from that anytime soon, if at all from the way he lay on the floor. The mirror with

Mackenzie etched in acid lay as shattered as it's namesake in the room in front of him. To make the situation worse, the spirits sprayed across the bar and walls. The candles flared bright blue as the alcohol ran down the wall and into the sconces. Flames licked across the wall and danced upon the liquor.

"Shit!" Karl exclaimed as his fears tripled in front of him. "This is the last God damned thing we need."

Marie screamed but it was cut off mid-yell. He threw himself into the door only to bounce off of it. He tried again and received a sore shoulder for his efforts. Instead of a third attempt, he pulled his rifle off his back and blew a hole in the door and frame where the lock had been. He kicked the door and it flew open. Marie lay on the floor. Her throat torn out in a ragged wound. Her left arm was snapped in half at the elbow. Her dress was torn open and it appeared her heart had been ripped out of her chest. The Wendigo was nowhere to be seen but the door to the outside balcony was open. He ran out into the night and saw the monster leap through a window into the next room. Karl ran past it and ducked his head as shots were fired, praying a stray bullet didn't hit him. He saw Otto spin with a fountain of blood erupting from where his face had been. Frank was backed against the door trying desperately to reload his shotgun.

He looked in the next room and saw it was empty and kept moving, hoping against hope Jia-Li and Mikhail were in the last one. He got to the window and barely avoided the shot that came through the glass.

Mikhail realized it was him and opened the door.

"What the hell are you doing out here?" he whispered. "I could have killed you."

"C'mon. It's down the hall still. We can climb down here if we are quick."

Jia-Li came out and touched Karl's cheek gently. Her eyes were filled with tears. Mikhail helped her over the railing and she scurried down the heavy corner beam with surprising grace. Mikhail looked at Karl who motioned for him to go. Mikhail didn't have quite the same effortlessness but made it down with a few grunts and groans. Karl lifted his leg to follow when the door to the room they had just vacated splintered open. Karl stared at the black eyes of the Wendigo. Its flesh was covered in gore and streaks of black ichor. It smiled at him and he felt his bowels shudder.

"Aaaaaaaaaaaat laaaaaaaasssssstttt"

Karl gulped as it ran towards him. He looked down at Mikhail and Jia-Li watching each other and staring in horror at him. "Ruuuuuuuuun!" he screamed.

And then he felt the impact as the Wendigo launched itself into him. The railing cracked, as did his left femur, and pain burst through his side. He wrapped his arms around the Wendigo's and they both went over the edge. He somehow managed to use the force of the creature to spin enough that he landed on top of it. He rolled off of it and lay still on the ground as the beating he had taken left his entire body wracked with agony. He felt his breaths come in wheezes and the telltale signs of broken ribs. The creature lay still beside him. He reached for his gun, but it wasn't on his side. He felt around on the ground but it wasn't within reach. The Wendigo began to twitch next to him and he just stared at the stars above.

Then he heard the crunch of footsteps and lifted his head to see Mikhail and Jia-Li standing front of him. Jia-Li raised her shotgun and shot the Wendigo point blank in the face. The sound was deafening at such close range and he felt the remains of the head splatter against his face. She took her time and reloaded. Mikhail grabbed Karl by the shoulders and dragged him away. Again the shotgun exploded into the night. And again. And again.

"You gonna be alright there, Hoss?" Mikhail asked with concern.

"Told you to run."

"You think you can tell the missus what to do? You're a damn bigger fool than I had previously believed." He laughed and propped Karl up against a barrel. "Baby, I think you got it." He called out to Jia-Li.

Another shot rang out in the night which sounded funny in Karl's ears. He added concussion to his list of injuries. He watched as the happy couple picked up chunks of the Wendigo and began tossing them into the fire that raged through Kenzie's. The blood red writing began to blacken as the flames slowly ate their way up the outside wall.

Let the bastard come back from that.

Jia-Li had quite literally blown it to pieces with a surgeon-like efficiency. They tossed limbs and then finally the torso and bits of head that remained into the fire. A smile formed on Karl's bloody and battered face through the pain and then the world went black.

EPILOGUE

DUNCAN

THE RIDER REINED his horse as he got to the center of the one-road town. He looked at the mess that greeted him with a scowl. One side of town was nothing but burnt timber. Even the church was nothing but a charred steeple on barely standing timbers, gutted by whatever had started the fire. He got off his horse and tied it in front of the general store.

"Hello!" he shouted. Only his echo rang out in greeting.

He peeked his head into the store and shouted again. Nothing. He looked about and found that it had been thoroughly ransacked. His hand went to the weapon on his hip as he walked down the street. All of the building that remained, a damn sight too few from what he had been told to expect, were empty. He walked to the end of the road and saw a small house, a quaint little thing really, and went to the door and knocked. As his fist hit the wood, it opened up. He stepped in cautiously. It was as abandoned as the rest of the town. He looked around and his eyes landed on a bloody paper on the table. Old blood, he noticed. At least a week or so. He picked up and read the carefully written words.

Of Monsters and Men, Hunger on the Chisholm Trail by Cody 'Sawbones' Higgins.

"What in tarnation is this supposed to mean?" he asked softly. Next to the paper, he saw the glint of metal. The sheriff's star he had come to town to receive sat in front of him. He picked it up and looked it over. Then he tossed it back on the table and shut the door behind him. He got back on his horse and shook his head in disbelief before trotting it over to a water pump. He filled the trough and washed the dirt off of his face as his horse drank thirstily.

"Looks like we came all this way for nothing, girl. Whatddya say? Head back or keep moving West?"

The horse ignored him as it drank and he pulled out a brush and began to clean the dust off of its flanks.

"West it is, then. No need for a sheriff in a ghost town."

ABILENE

Karl lay in bed staring out the window. Mikhail and Jia-Li sat quietly at the table to his side.

"You sure?" Mikhail asked for the thirtieth time.

"Take your beautiful wife and get on that goddamned train already. I'm fine. You've got an address to send me a letter once you are settled. In a couple of weeks, I'll be back to my old ways and head up to Wisconsin. Once I finish my business there, I'll head East and then take a train out to see you. I don't know how many times I can explain this until it sinks into your thick skull."

"Leave him be, Pup. He has his own journey, just as we have ours."

Mikhail shook his head. "A fool's errand. Chasing Luck. You could pan for gold with us. Retire. Find yourself a pretty lady and settle down."

Karl didn't look at him. "It isn't for me. It's to save the world. Besides, pretty ladies and I don't tend to work out so well."

"You didn't know what was gonna happen in Duncan. None of us did. We barely survived, wouldn't have without your help. Blasted idiot. The offer stands." Mikhail's eyes were softer than his words betrayed.

"Tell him!" Jia-Li said excitedly.

"Tell me what? If it is another ploy to lure me out into a river looking like a moron with a pan, I swear . . . "

"She is pregnant."

"What?"

"Jia-Li is pregnant."

"How?"

"We had sex. Mikhail and I. It was quite lovely. See, a couple months ago he came home in a foul mood. Tense. And I realized the best way to relieve his stress was to have . . . "

"Damn it, I know how it happened. How long have you known?"

Mikhail laughed. "She told me as we tossed bits of

the Wendigo into the fire. You had gone to sleep already."

"Two weeks! You've known for two weeks and just now tell me?"

"You were otherwise busy sulking. Didn't want to ruin your mood." Jia-Li smiled and rose. She gave him a fond kiss on the cheek. "If it is a boy, we name him Karl Benjamin. If it is a girl, she will be Tracey Rose."

Karl looked at her with a smile. He felt the tears roll down his cheek. "She would have loved that. And I am honored."

"Now will you come with us?" Mikhail ducked as Karl threw a boot at him. "Fine. You ornery old cuss. Don't say I didn't ask. We are leaving this afternoon. Your cut of the cash from the Post Office safe is here. You change your mind and we will be in San Francisco for a few months as we research land grants and good spots to prospect."

"Good luck to you. To both of you. I'll be out by the time the baby is born, I hope. Try not to make a mess of things before I get there."

TRIBAL LANDS, INDIAN REGION

The former nearly sheriff rode slowly over the ridge. Laid out in front of him were the tents of the Tribes. He stopped his horse and stared intently. There was no movement as far as he could see. It wasn't like them to leave their things unattended like this. He heeled his horse and made his way in. The smell of death was strong, and his horse rolled its eyes in terror as he forced it deeper in. He patted her neck and whistled low into the silence.

"What happened here, girl?"

Blood splattered the hides that whipped about in the wind.

"Looks like a slaughter."

As he rode, he began to hear the sound of someone digging and he kept on as it grew louder. A lone Indian stood bare chested. Around him were hundreds of graves and, by the look of him, he had dug them all. The Indian turned and stared at him.

"They all take sick?"

The Indian shook his head.

"What happened? Same thing that happened at Duncan?"

The Indian dropped his shovel. "What happened at Duncan?"

"Hell if I know. I rode into town this morning and half the town was ash and the other half abandoned."

The Indian dropped his head into his hands and gave an anguished scream.

"Mind telling me what the hell is going on?"

River looked up at the man, tears streaming down his face. "We were too late. Too cocky. And everyone died because of it."

"What the hell does that mean?"

"Hasse Ola, my friend and brother, did this. The ritual was too late. The taint of his father was too strong."

"The taint?"

He looked at the stranger with empty eyes.

"Wendigo. His father destroyed Duncan. And here Hasse Ola gave in as well. Be wary stranger. Somewhere out there," he pointed in a circle outward, "at least one Wendigo roams the plains."

The man stared without understanding then clucked his tongue and heeled his mare. "Damn Savages. Make no sense at all."

As he rode away, he heard the sounds of digging behind him begin again.

THE END

ABOUT THE AUTHOR

M Ennenbach roams the wilderness alone with his trusty six shooter and a horse named Girl. A poet, author and madman; he sings punk rock around the campfire to annoy the monsters. One third of Cerberus, the greatest collective ever assembled. He insists upon world domination.